Piranha Frenzy

By Colin Campbell

Colin Campbell

Video game journalist Kjersti Wong has just a few hours to
complete the big review of summer blockbuster *Satanic Realm 5*
for her employer, big games website Piranha Frenzy.
Kjersti's bosses, the game's fans and even her partner are
pressuring her to deliver a high score. But there's something
about this game that is deeply troubling. Her investigations
and actions over the next few hours will change her life, and
the world of gaming, forever.

Colin Campbell

ACKNOWLEDGMENTS

Thanks to my wonderful wife Maryanne who offered so much help

and support during the writing of this book. Also, thanks to my editor

Carrie Shepherd who did a great job knocking this into shape. Thanks

also to those kind individuals who read the book prior to publication,

and offered amazingly useful insights, and to my

admirable friends and colleagues at Polygon.

Colin Campbell

Editor: Carrie Shepherd
Designer: Maryanne Campbell
Copyright © 2014 Colin Campbell
All rights reserved.
ISBN: 9780615948225

CONTENTS

CHARACTERS

SHELDON TAVERNIER - Publisher
Born: Petersham, Massachusetts, 1975
Favorite Game: The Legend of Zelda: Ocarina of Time

BRAD HOFFMAN - Editor-in-Chief
Born: San Diego, California, 1982
Favorite Game: "Anything with badass guns."

STEVE CARTER - Senior Editor
Born: Burbank, California, 1984
Favorite Game: Grand Theft Auto 6

FRANK ARNOLD - Managing Editor
Born: Adelaide, Australia, 1959
Favorite Game: "Roosters vs. Bulldogs, 1971."

ANGIE JONES - Producer
Born: Chicago, Illinois, 1979
Favorite Game: Journey

KJERSTI WONG - Head Presenter
Born: Oslo, Norway, 1982
Favorite Game: Satanic Realm

CHARLIE BLACK - News Writer
Born: St. Louis, Missouri, 1992
Favorite Game: Atelier Iris - Eternal Mana

ZOE ZELLER - Junior Writer
Born: San Luis Obispo, California, 1995
Favorite Game: "Really difficult puzzles."

LIAM SULLIVAN - Presenter
Born: Cork, Ireland, 1987
Favorite Game: The Elder Scrolls Online

And...
ALEJANDRO BERNAL - Chief Marketing Officer, Saturnine
Born: Santa Fe, New Mexico, 1976
Favorite Game: "Everything Saturnine makes."

1

FIGURINES

8:15 a.m.

Kjersti Wong gazes at the crawling hell-scape. Groaning imps patrol in musical patterns, throbbing portals glow crimson.

Her character, a spangled female mage, strikes an expectant stance of readiness. At the corner of the screen, burnished clouds conceal an unknown prize: the correct path, a final, elusive puzzle.

Kjersti checks the game clock and makes some notes on a laptop. She's been playing *Satanic Realm 5* for more than twenty-four hours. The game's end draws near.

So too, the review embargo. She wants—needs—to rest her eyes, but she must complete the game before she can write her verdict.

Through the blinds at the far end of the office, L.A. sunlight cuts into the great room, illuminating gray equipment, garish promotional posters and a horde of figurines—Pokémon, Marvel, Disney, Elder Scrolls, Final Fantasy—a visual language of identity for the staffers at Piranha Frenzy, one of video gaming's biggest online news outlets.

At the corners of her own desk sit two family photos in simple frames, equidistant.

She wonders if it might have been wiser to have played the game on her rig at home. But at the house-share, she always has to deal with the chaos of her housemates.

Kjersti's job is a glamorous but low-yield position in game media. She isn't paid enough to afford an apartment of her own. The threat of her teeming house keeps her office-bound, working the necessary hours to complete in a few days a game designed to last at least fifty hours from start to end. Here, at least, she can focus on playing.

The first editorial workers of the day, the usual early-bird oddballs, make their way to open-plan cubicles. Keyboards begin to clack.

A shabby man takes his place at a desk opposite Kjersti: Frank Arnold, mid-50s, grey-blond hair sprouting from all the wrong places.

He is wearing wrinkled chinos and a badly frayed Havana jacket. He begins work, says nothing. Peering through bushy eyebrows, he frowns at his screen and indulges a habit of constipated groaning as he moves through Piranha Frenzy's overnight copy.

"Incomprehensible drivel," he mutters. "Garbled nonsense."

Kjersti is aware that it shouldn't be too long before she's able to figure out the *Satanic Realm 5* endgame puzzle, reach the final boss, kill it and settle into the bigger problem of writing the review. But she's tired of looking at the screen, at the mage and the churning brimstone fantasy. So she stares at Frank and waits for him to acknowledge her. She's been here all night, alone. She wants to talk to a human being.

"Need any help with that review, Kjersti?" he asks, finally looking up.

He is the only one who pronounces her name with its proper Norwegian inflection, a slight turn on the J, "Kee-ursty." To everyone else in this country, she is "Kirsty."

"It's a fine art you know, reviewing," he smirks. "It takes finesse, delicacy..."

His accent is Australian, his voice, unmistakably, that of a man who has spent many years smoking cigarettes.

"I'm fine," she says, smiling, allowing him his easy bantering.

"You sure, Kjersti? It's a lot harder than standing in front of a video camera, looking cute and reading a script."

Now she laughs. Frank is the only person at the office who would get away with a jab like that, and even then, only in private.

"Actually, I do have a question," she says, pointing at her keyboard.

"The big long button without any letters on it?" She places a finger on her lips in mock-coquetry. "What does it do?"

"Ah," he says, crossing his fingers magisterially. "I believe that is the shoot button, my flower. For making the nasty monsters go away."

"The shoot button?" She guffaws. A few heads pop up from cubicles.

"You're an idiot, Frank."

"Pow," he fires at her, smiling. "Fire, blam-de-blam. Everyone is dead. Hurrah for the video games."

"Aw, that's cute," she says. "Is this where you make that speech of yours? The one about the game biz being the most interesting industry in the whole wide world, except for the trash they actually produce?"

"You've heard that one?"

"Only a dozen times," she says. "Games are great. The people who sell them? Maybe less so."

"Well," he says, with a theatrical grin of self-satisfaction. "I suppose you'd have inside knowledge of that."

She doesn't find this funny. Not at all. He sees her reaction, and his face falls. Before he can reach for an apology, she offers a significant look over his shoulder, juts her chin out. It's a signal that the editor-in-chief has arrived. Frank's shoulders slump slightly. Kjersti can't tell if this is a reaction to his own clumsy faux pas about her love life, or the arrival of their boss.

She rubs her face, runs a hand through her short hair and bunches it at the back, prepares to adopt a facial expression suggesting the basic hierarchical respect toward the incoming EIC.

Brad Hoffman, editor-in-chief, is all bicycle helmet and ankle clips, face sweaty and red. He bounds up to Frank, places his hands on the older man's shoulders, prompting another reaction of physical discomfort in the Australian. The shoulders go up, hover tortuously a few inches south of his enormous, grizzled earlobes.

"Morning everyone," booms Brad. "Big, big day today. Huge. Massive." He is standing directly behind Frank, almost leaning on him. "I've been cramming on *Satanic Realm 5*. Kjersti, it looks awesome. Can't wait to play."

He places an extraordinary emphasis on the "awe" in "awesome" while flicking the "some" out like a lash, a verbal pretense that has attracted no shortage of late-night imitative cacophonies in the editorial department's favored drinking establishments.

Kjersti catches a wry smile from Frank who opens his mouth wide, in a semi-yawn that also suggests an "awe," the mocking in-office comedy keyword.

She ignores this, moves her game controller to activate the mage, replies flatly. "The last campaign will be finished soon. I'll have everything ready in good time."

Brad jumps up and moves around the bank of desks, stands beside her. She hopes he doesn't touch her shoulders. He studies the screen of Kjersti's laptop—a stream of Norwegian. Kjersti always keeps notes in her native language.

"I haven't decided the score yet," she says, anticipating the EIC's reason for standing by her desk, craning his neck in a futile attempt to decode her text.

Brad perches on the edge of her desk, forcing her to scuttle her chair a few inches out of his way. He always wears dark sunglasses and sports a hyper-neatly trimmed goatee. She finds her eyes drawn down his long face, to the goatee's strange motions. As he speaks, she watches it move, revealing the soft pinkness of his mouth. At these moments, she is always touched by a faint revulsion. Secretly, she has given the goatee a private name of its own, a Pokémon name, "Caprabullo".

He has worn the same goatee for years, had opted for this particular facial hair formation just at the point when such a look had reached its high-point in the fashion subdivision of professional-men-in-creative industries and, having made his investment so late in the game, she assumes, he is loathe to move on. Caprabullo is here to stay.

"Oh hey, Charlie..." Brad raises an arm to wave at a young man crossing the office toward them, weaving between the lines of fantasy-festooned desks. The young man, speaking into a cell phone, returns the barest of greetings.

"Nintendo is planning this at G2G?" the young man says into the phone, as he dumps his backpack and takes a seat at the desk next to Kjersti. "No, that's not possible. That's not their MO at all." His tone is conspiratorial, newsy, vaguely comedy-French, even though he's from someplace in the Midwest.

The EIC looks back at Kjersti, claps his hands together. "So, *Satanic Realm 5*. Embargo drops in a few hours. Any clues for the old EIC?" Kjersti is mildly irritated by Brad's use of the word "old," his attempt to assert seniority. They were both born the same year, 1982. "Big day today. Not a good day for surprises," he says.

Frank looks up from his work, frowns. "We still have protocols about reviewers not having to reveal scores, right, Brad?"

"Au revoir," says Charlie Black, breathing into his phone, almost whispering. He pockets his phone and now all three of them at the bank of desks are looking at the EIC, waiting for a reply.

"Yes, yes, of course," says Brad, showing his palms, fingers spread. The intended effect of authenticity is hindered somewhat, by his wearing of sunglasses indoors. "Protocols. It's just good to know the score, you know, me being the editor-in-chief. Planning... Crazy, crazy, busy day. G2G is upon us, people."

There's a moment's shared discomfort. Brad stands up. The staffers look at him. Then Charlie speaks. "Nintendo. Definitely announcing something. Tomorrow, at G2G."

Frank sighs, puts his coffee down. "A limited-edition twentieth anniversary Nintendo 64, made entirely of marzipan? Impeccable sources, no doubt."

Brad throws Frank a look of annoyance. "What is it?" he says to Charlie. "Can it be verified by three sources?"

Kjersti has heard Brad mention, on at least 20 occasions, that he took a media course at college. He always jumps enthusiastically into these moments when it's possible to pretend that Piranha Frenzy circles noble orbits of journalism.

Charlie stares back, says nothing. He is, thinks Kjersti, a strange lad, short and deathly pale with dyed black hair, almost purple, heavily stylized like a JRPG cloud-warrior, to which his clothes, large mauve lapels and angular flaps, pay homage.

"My source works at an ad agency in Paris," Charlie says. "She's been working on some artwork for..." He pauses and stands up. Kjersti isn't sure if this is one of his perplexingly unfunny jokes, or a moment of unironic grandiosity.

"Nintendo Readying Next F-Zero." He declares the headline as if he is a TV anchor.

"Pssshaw. That rumor's been around for years," says Frank. "Of course Nintendo is announcing something. It's the biggest show of the year. It's Nintendo. It's the twentieth anniversary of Nintendo 64. Try again. Try Pilot Wings or maybe Custom Robo. Just as likely. You're guessing, Charlie."

Frank has never played those video games. He never plays games. But his industry knowledge is encyclopedic. "We can't afford any fuck-ups," he says. "If we run this and it doesn't happen, we'll look like morons. Again."

Brad is stroking his chin. "It's a big story. Lots of interest. Traffic. You say this source is good? Can you tell us more?"

Kjersti tunes out; the spectacle of these machismo newsroom fantasies depresses her. Guys like Brad are forever standing at the center, while she is a junior, an ornament, a token, mostly humored, certainly not considered for the awesome responsibility of editor-in-chiefdom, which apparently consists of standing around, failing to come to a decision, playing at Woodward and Bernstein over the next fucking racer from Nintendo. It pisses her off.

She returns to her mage, tries double-backing with her character to look for levers or hidden triggers. The map is familiar. Her annoyance with the surrounding newsroom buffoonery fades as a sense comes to her, one that she has been grappling with all night, that she knows exactly where she'll find a hidden portal that will unlock the puzzle. A schematic forms in her mind.

This feeling of déjà vu has dogged her throughout the game. She keeps seeing motifs, visual jokes and characters that seem familiar, that hark back to a distant past, that somehow don't quite fit the Satanic Realm mythos. Is her own fatigue affecting her judgment?

She works her way back to the point where she believes she can progress, ignores invitations to battle from meowing shrubbery, bobby socked mushrooms and twisted inside-out babies. She needs to find a landmark; a rainbow touches her mind. How is it possible that she has done this before? The designers of the game can't have made the endgame-puzzle a repeat of something earlier in the game, can they?

She tries to remember, reminds herself that she has been playing for almost 24 hours straight, that her life and her living depend on her spending thousands upon thousands of hours playing games, or looking at videos of them, or reading stories about them or listening to her co-workers talk about them.

Writing about video games is not a normal way to make a living. "Maybe I've just played too many games," she thinks.

Frank is speaking to Brad, his voice raised slightly, "We're not talking about some vague future event, we're talking about an alleged Nintendo announcement tomorrow. I call bollocks."

"But we can't ignore this source," says Brad. "Can we get someone else to stack it up? An analyst, maybe?"

Frank snorts. "Let's be honest. It's not as if Charlie here has the best of records, even with his 'high-level contacts'."

"Have it your way, Frank," says Charlie. "But when this happens, or it gets broken by NeoGAF or Kotaku..."

Brad groans the groan of an editor anticipating the heat he'll take if he sits on a genuine scoop. Kjersti hopes the posturing will end so Brad and his dark sunglasses and Caprabullo can leave them alone and she can finish the game. She follows a path with her mage. She enters a building, a forge of some sort. There is a sparkling rainbow within—a strange juxtaposition, almost crude but charming, somehow unlike the Satanic Realm canon.

"This game is weirding me out," she thinks.

"Charlie, man, do what you can to make it stand up, and run the story," says Brad. He walks toward his own desk in the corner of the great room.

"And Kjersti, I want the copy on my desk by lunchtime." He is speaking more sharply now. His tussle with Frank has erased the morning's collegial chumminess.

"Have a score ready for me by the morning meeting. Let's not make today any more difficult than it needs to be."

Kjersti says nothing. There it is: a trapdoor, guarded by dancing hippo skeletons. She shoos them away; something tells her not to kill them. It's the right thing to do. They morph into a key. She drops into the trapdoor. After a few moments of traversing obstacles, crossing bridges and slaughtering curious little imps, the screen dissolves to a large platform, at the center of which stands an enormous manifestation of Satan.

"I'm sorry about that remark earlier. It was crass of me."

She turns to see Frank crouching beside her on the floor, leaning in. She catches a smell of liniment. She can't shake this old habit of smelling him, just in case he's fallen off the wagon.

"It's OK," she says. "I'm used to it by now." Her relationship with a powerful video game exec is common knowledge, the stuff of endless barbs.

"Yes, but the difference is… It upsets me to sound like one of these assholes," says Frank, gesturing at the office. "You know that, right?"

"I'm fine. I forgive you Frank. Really," she gives him a smile, which she hopes he'll take as a signal that she's far too busy to salve his bruised feelings.

"I'm worried about you, Kjersti," says Frank. "You're in an invidious situation. I know you're a big girl…" She raises an eyebrow at him. He falters. "…I know you can handle yourself, but I don't see how you can come out of this well. You can only be hurt by writing this review."

"I get it, Frank," she sighs. "We've been over this. I'll review the game on its own merits. That's it."

"I know. It's just…"

"Those assholes?"

"Yeah."

Frank is the only one who has supported her requests to review big games—"triple A" in the industry vernacular. For years, the editors refused to even acknowledge her requests to show that she could review competently. You're on the video side, they said, with apparent sincerity— and video presenters don't review games.

But eventually, they relented and gave her a game to review: *Mindy's Make-Up Simulator*. She had performed well, so they had offered her *Pony Dreams* followed by a couple of Facebook social games and, finally, *Dance Sensation 9*.

That's when she'd gone to the publisher and begged him to allow her to review "a proper game," like *Satanic Realm 4*, hinting in the vaguest possible terms of a potential escalation into the realms of an HR complaint.

Brad had allowed it, but pitching for reviews was still an exercise in frustration. She sighs and faces Frank. "I'll tell you something," she says quietly. "Brad came to me last week and asked if I might use my influence to get an exclusive for the review."

"Because you're dating Alejandro Bernal?"

"He didn't say as much. He was like, if I thought I was going to enjoy the game, if it looked like there would be a positive score, we might be able to figure something out with Saturnine—an exclusive review."

"Very cozy. And you said?"

"I said I don't agree with exclusive reviews and I had no idea what the score would be anyway. I said that I had to tread very carefully, because my relationship with Alejandro is very public. Brad looked pissed but he dropped it, thank goodness."

"I don't know why you took this game," says Frank. "It's poison. You're dating the man who is marketing the bloody thing. It's wrong. Why do it?"

"Because, Frank, no one knows this series as well as I do. Because I reviewed the last game in the series, and everyone knows I did a great job. Because I've been reviewing games since I was 12, but Brad and the others..."

"I know," he nods. "But..."

She throws him a look that says she doesn't want to hear it, not again. The bosses gave her this game to review because they know she's solid on this one series, because she gave *Satanic Realm 4* a high score, and maybe because they think she just might be corrupt enough to want to curry favor with her boyfriend.

When Brad offered it, she knew all of this, but still she took the review, because they hardly ever trust her with big reviews. The last game they gave her was a crappy HD remake of a 1995 platformer about cutesy alligators.

She wants to prove that no one will review this game better than she will.

"If I don't start getting serious about reviewing these big bastard games, I'm never going to get beyond, as you say, looking cute in front of a camera."

"If you give the game a good score, they'll say you're in the thrall of your evil beau, the flashy marketing big shot at Saturnine. And if you give it a shitty score..."

"All hell breaks loose."

"In a manner of speaking."

She smiles. "That doesn't even factor in the fanboys." It's been publicly known for a week or two that she will be reviewing the game for Piranha Frenzy, and the Satanic Realm faithful have already been on the message boards debating whether it'll get a perfect score.

"Ah yes, the boy fanatics," Creakily, Frank lifts himself up. "Just so long as you know, I'm here to help."

"I know," she says.

Kjersti turns back to Satan. She unpauses the game and begins casting spells. She thinks about the review score. The fans, the bosses and the publisher will be expecting something north of 85%. They will express deep and terrible anger if she scores the game lower than 80%.

The Metacritic average, she thinks, will be around 83%. She has learned the knack of fairly accurately predicting a game's average review score, long before the review copies are sent out. She is not always right, but not often wrong.

The buzz about this game has been mostly positive. It's not designed to change the world, but it is a known quantity. To Kjersti though, the realization has arrived that there's something wrong with this game.

Something urgent, but nonobvious.

Usually, when a game is bad, the awfulness leaks out: exchanged glances from journalists at preview events, little digs on Twitter. This game has had nothing but good press, even though preview events have been highly controlled, with reporters allowed to play only for short periods on specific levels, under constant supervision.

Review copies were sent out late, usually a bad sign. But it's clear that the game is slick, smooth, professionally mustered. Everything looks, sounds and plays as it should. It's just irritating her in a way she cannot explain. It keeps needling some part of her memory, something deep and unreachable. She has no idea what she's going to say in her review.

Kjersti glances at the photographs on her desk, one of her mother and one of her father. A memory stirs within her, a strange connection between the present and the past, a brief puzzle that passes before she can fully register its relevance. She thinks of her dad playing games, selecting his favorites from tidy, well-organized boxes of CDs, cartridges, floppies and cassettes. The memory makes her smile. It always does.

The one thing that she knows for sure is that she doesn't like this game, and doesn't want to give it anything like 85%. She spell-casts a shower of ice-shards over Satan. He isn't happy.

2

OH

10:38 a.m.

Kjersti is waved into the studio by Piranha Frenzy's producer, Angie Jones, seated at a control console, looking as bored as any checkout jockey.

In the center of the room, three men, all in their mid-to-late twenties, all wearing jeans and T-shirts, are lounging in easy chairs, facing one another at tables decked out with mic rigs, laptops and other podcasting junk. They're talking, broadcasting live on audio and video, so she enters quietly and takes the empty seat. She knows how this is done.

The men are debating *Satanic Realm 5*. They're talking it up as a potential game of the year, before it's even been released. They are talking about how *Satanic Realm 4*'s multiplayer online battle arena mode has turned pro gaming upside down in the past year, creating yet another schism between adherents of one game over another, a divisive and nasty war of words that's worse than anyone can remember.

The days when gamers identified with hardware like Genesis, PlayStation or PC are drawing to a close. Now they identify with genres or even individual games, sometimes fanatically. The worst of them have become like sports fans or political ideologues.

Debates about video games are now fertile ground for cynical rabble-rousers, trolls, traffic-hounds and click-bait headline-writers.

She smiles at the podcasters and at the camera, tries to hide her mounting anxiety. She still hasn't written a word of the *Satanic Realm 5* review, the daily morning meeting is less than thirty minutes away, and she has this irritating podcast interview to complete.

The show's host is Steve Carter. He speaks into a fat mic.

"Yeah, so I guess Satanic Realm, we all love it, but it has always courted controversy, been a focus for the usual haters in the mass media," he says. "The violence thing is just typical fear-mongering from the usual elites. They don't seem to get that games are fantasies and fantasies are always violent but not the same as real-life violence. Not at all."

His two co-hosts nod agreeably. Behind them, silent cardboard standees of gaming icons are artfully lighted and in the midst of doing their thing: Mario jumps, Sonic runs, Dovahkiin roars, Lara shoots.

There is also one of Kjersti, posing with a Nintendo DS, mocking fear with Donkey Kong bearing down from behind. She is ten years younger. The standee embarrasses her now. It makes her feel like a cartoon, a video game character, designed to bounce across primary-colored platforms, avoiding turtles. Even then, she knew she was too old for this '80s photo-strip cartoon nonsense.

Steve continues speaking, recording-voice smile on his face. He has high school quarterback looks; tight, auburn curls, a slight chunkiness in his torso, suggesting golf-course girth in the years to come.

"So, we're nearly at the end of this week's show, also video-streaming live to you right now via the Internet's magical tubes, but we've got so much more this week, with G2G happening tomorrow..."

Kjersti listens to this show every week, not because she wants to, but because, as the network's primary video presenter, she likes to know every last thing the network creates—every podcast, news feature, tweet and screenshot-upload.

"And now we have the lovely Kjersti Wong, veteran Internet starlet, joining us to talk about her video news show. How are you, Kjersti?"

She tries not to wince at this intro. "I'm delighted to have been invited on to your fantastic show."

Every person in the room knows that Kjersti has never been invited on to this show, which is the preserve of Carter and his cronies. Marketing has suggested, via mass company email, that "cross-pollination of media assets are maximized," during the G2G period, and Brad, always alive to Marketing's concerns, has dutifully set up the final ten-minute segment of the podcast to include Kjersti, whose own video show is a prime corporate asset.

"Well, uh, not really my show," says Carter. He raises a shot glass of liquor, toasts the room, drinks. "I like to think of it as being for the ages, so to speak."

This man-child is the heir apparent to the EIC's chair, she thinks. He has been here no longer than I have. Yet he is at least two levels above me in the hierarchy.

"I love that you're getting into the party mood already, Steve," she says, more brightly than she feels. "Courvoisier. Classy. And it's not even 11 a.m."

He tips his glass toward her, then winks into a camera.

"I hope you're going to be standing up straight tonight," she says. "Long day ahead." She wags her finger and beams. There are three cameras, and she's on two of them. She is required to look amiable.

"Don't worry about me," says Steve, not looking at Kjersti. "This cognac was sent to us by..." he shuffles through a pile of printouts... "some dude, can't find his name. Some days we get chocolate cake from our listeners and some days we get cognac. I guess I just roll with the punches."

Whooping from the cronies. She smiles politely. She disapproves of hosts receiving gifts from listeners and has said so in a number of media-department meetings, always though, howled down by the defense that Piranha Frenzy is all about being the gamer's friend, and friends exchange gifts. She is here to keep the podcast audience sweet. Steve and his sidekicks are popular and, with the review of *Satanic Realm 5* about to drop, she knows she could be in the middle of a fanboy shit-storm by the end of the day.

Whether she likes it or not, Steve represents something magical to the audience, idealized, imaginary versions of themselves, sipping free cognac in a recording studio, getting paid to blab about games, thousands of Twitter followers. Steve represents the collective aspirational alternative to their grinding struggle to find jobs in warehouse retail outlets, coffee shops and fast-food restaurants.

The podcast audience numbers are less than ten percent of Kjersti's YouTube show, which is syndicated across console platforms, various mobile deals, and sponsored by a cell-phone provider. But the podcast listeners are the fanatical Republican Guard of Piranha Frenzy's audience.

They are the sort of young men—always young men—who turn up chanting fanboy slogans at live events, the sort of people whose boisterous enthusiasm impresses outsiders, who inevitably compare them to college sports fans. These listeners make a lot of noise on the Internet and can be roused to defend what they see as their birthright, as carriers of the true flag of video gaming fandom.

She knows from the comments she reads on the Internet that this audience doesn't trust her—sees her as a fake, an interloper.

"So what's your plans for G2G, Kjersti? What can we expect from Gaming with Kjersti Wong this week?" She catches something unfriendly in Steve's voice.

Smoothly, she goes into autopilot. "I'll be on the show floor for the whole event, schmoozing with exhibitors, interviewing the top developers, broadcasting live as well as recording an hour-long special version of the show every day..." She picks her way through the pre-prepped BS, keeping her eyes smiling.

One of the co-hosts nudges the other. They are looking at messages from the audience. She's glad she isn't reading them. The violent, sexualized slurs she receives on her own show's comments are bad enough.

"...I've been coming to G2G for years, and it never stops being exciting," she says. "This being the twentieth anniv..."

"Yeah. There's always a lot of media attention on game journalists at this time of year," Carter interrupts, without looking up.

She suppresses a sigh. Steve's show spends way more time talking about game journalism than games. Like most of its genre, it is a game podcast in which game journalists talk about themselves.

"And you yourself have been the focus of a lot of scrutiny," Steve continues. "I mean when you were younger."

She pauses, smiles with what she hopes is a veneer of patience. "This? Again, Steve? Really?"

"Oh, hey, Kjersti. I'm sorry to bring it up. I know it's a touchy subject. But it's a listener question just come in on the Tweeter."

She knows she's going to have to tell the story again, the tale that follows and humiliates her every day.

"Well, 'Oh' happened seven years ago, Steve," she says, uttering his name with poorly concealed contempt. "About 15 million people have watched the video on YouTube now, and the photo meme has been seen by countless millions more in endless variety. I've talked about it a hundred times.

"It changed my life in many ways, good and bad. I don't know what I can add. It was just one of those things."

She'd been sat at a demo of *Call of Duty: Modern Warfare 2*, seven years before. A PR rep gave her a controller. She played with it for a few seconds. Just as she realized that she was not controlling onscreen events, that it was on auto-loop, that the controller wasn't connected, just as she was about to put the controller down, a man had stepped in and gently taken it out of her hands.

She'd looked up, surprised, and said, "Oh."

That was the video. A camera pointed up at her, an unflattering angle, the sweat and stress of the day upon her face and neck. The room had been crowded with journalists. She never knew who filmed it, or who leaked it.

"Oh" was the word that named the whole thing. Oh.

Her turned head, the game blurred in the background, her mouth in the shape of an "O," her look of confusion and embarrassment—that was the image-meme, pasted with barbs and wisecracks in white block letters, Photoshopped in an endless parade of video game- or pop culture-themed backgrounds. She was the clueless girl who just didn't get that which was obvious to the true believers.

Even today, people pointed at her at PAX, Comic-Con, G2G and even in the street and yelled "Oh" and laughed. A few times, she had been introduced by influential people at industry parties—subsequently mortified by their error—as "Kjersti Oh."

Nobody cared to hear that Modern Warfare 2 had been the twenty-third game she'd looked at in ten hours, that she was exhausted. What mattered was that she seemed not to know what the hell she was doing. She became the poster chick for the archetype of dumb wannabe geek-girls, a favored target of Steve's show and of Steve's audience.

"Oh" was one of the top five virals of 2009. It destroyed her credibility among the hardcore, while at the same time making her the most recognizable face in game journalism. There were many who defended her, pointed out the circumstance, that it was a mistake anyone could have made. Had she been a man, it would have been laughed off as the result of too much partying the night before.

She survived, just, but it never left her. Over the years it had caused her confusion, anger and despair. She tried to laugh it off, publicly and to herself, without ever entirely succeeding.

"It must be tough for you." Steve gives her a Barbara Walters look of concern.

"Not really, Steve," she says trying to control the tone of her voice. "I know ten times more than anyone else in this room about games. That helps."

She only has a second to enjoy the look on his face, before the cronies start up a commotion. "Woah," comes from both the co-hosts. They're looking at their laptops. One of them booms, "Incoming."

"Eh, what's up?" says Carter.

"He's back," says one of the co-hosts. "The Scourge of Corruption is threatening to blog, tonight. At 8 p.m. Oh man. That's during the Piranha Frenzy G2G party."

The other co-host begins reading out loud. "The Scourge of Corruption has had enough of lies, bribery and craven cowardice in game journalism. We have evidence of outrageous wrongdoing at a leading outlet. Something very, very FISHY. Tonight you will all find out the truth."

"Not this guy again." says Steve Carter, his face flushed. "Hasn't he got anything else to worry about? Fucking prick."

There's a moment's dead air. Instinctively, Kjersti looks to Angie, who is mouthing silent oaths and slapping her forehead.

Swearing on live-streams is not allowed. It has been banned since the early days of Piranha Frenzy podcasting, since a newspaper in Texas kicked up a fuss about an unfortunate anecdote, recorded and transmitted, about a junior editor's boast that he had spent the weekend "fucking the bejeezus out of my cousin's stepmom."

"Well, he blogged about journalism for five years," she says, trying to rescue the situation. "Now he's had, what, eighteen months without a word? He probably just misses us."

Giggles from the cronies. Angie is making the "wrap-this-up" motion.

Kjersti wants to get on with her day. She has to attend the morning meeting, record her show, write the review and get down to the Los Angeles Convention Center to prepare for tomorrow's live G2G broadcasts. Somewhere in there, she needs to take a shower and change her clothes.

She wants to see Alejandro, although she doesn't know why, or what she's going to say to him. "Oh hey, Alex. I really don't like your game, hope you don't mind your girlfriend shitting all over it," doesn't seem like it will achieve much.

For the past few hours. she's been grappling with the game's echoes of the past, trying to make a solid connection. But nothing has come to mind. Her notes offered no insight to the problem. When she completed the final mission, she loaded up her Word program and stared at a blank screen.

She can't slam the game just because it makes her feel weird. Nor, she feels, can she wholly recommend a product she doesn't like.

She's still bugged by the thought that the game carries a connection to the past. She needs to look at some of her archived blog posts covering earlier games in the series.

Carter wraps the show. He forgets to thank his guest, but Kjersti is out of her chair as soon as the camera switches away from her.

3

POPCORN

11:00 a.m.

Sheldon Tavernier, senior publisher of Piranha Frenzy, settles heavily into his great black leather chair, in his traditional location, close to the Big Meeting Room door.

An intern hands him a large bag of warm movie-house popcorn, extra buttery, before slipping through the door, dodging incoming journalists. Sheldon dislikes microwave popcorn, so every morning, he sends the intern out to a nearby movie theater for fresh.

Members of the editorial team file into the room and take their places for the Morning Meeting. Some sit in random seats, others favor special spots.

They are mostly men in their 20s or early 30s, and a few women. He smiles at them all, nods agreeably, eats his popcorn. Same routine. He has sat in meetings like this every day for years. The faces change, but not much.

Frank Arnold enters and takes his place at the far end of the room.

"Another busy day at the center of the gaming universe, eh, Frank?" says Sheldon, loudly enough for the hubbub of pre-meeting chatter to instantly dissolve. Mobile phones and iPads are stashed away. Sheldon doesn't tolerate gadgets in his meetings.

"Here's to The Scourge," says Frank, smiling and raising a chipped coffee cup. "And we all thought he'd retired, bless his black heart."

"Retired? He ought to be committed to an asylum."

"I see Twitter is ablaze with this. Any clue what he might be getting ready to unleash upon a quaking universe?"

Sheldon shrugs. "More lies, Frank. More lies."

Kjersti Wong arrives and sits, as always, next to Frank. Sheldon thinks she looks tired; certainly she has lost much of that sweet friskiness he used to enjoy so much in her. He ponders, not for the first time, if Frank's influence is the cause of her decline, and regrets ever seating them together in one of his world-changing office-furniture re-orgs.

Charlie Black stands by the wall, away from the main group. He looks as ridiculous as ever in one of his video game costumes. Sheldon contemplates teasing the boy, but remembers a recent HR-mandated online course about "aggressive humor paradigms in male-orientated creative environments" and decides to rest the knockabout boss routine. There's a lot to get through today, not least this goddamn nuisance, The Scourge of Corruption.

Steve Carter along with some of his chums sit together looking, to Sheldon's eye, reasonably normal, all wearing variations on a theme of fancily buttoned, fall-hued shirts, popular this year. He catches a faint whiff of liquor, and frowns.

Texting intently, Brad enters the room, sits down next to Sheldon, looking furiously engaged. He takes his sunglasses off, wipes his eyes.

"It might never happen, Brad," says Sheldon, grinning, sharing his joke with the room. Brad looks up, manages a smile. Sheldon secretly enjoys the spectacle of Brad looking harassed. It allows him, Sheldon, to appear effortlessly in control, even while he boils with rage at the prospect of a damaging blog post from a former employee.

On his resume, Brad had listed his biggest strength as "an upbeat and positive attitude," which Sheldon found quaint. He had resolved at the time to test this boast thoroughly and has enjoyed doing so. It is clear to Sheldon that Brad is openly freaking out about this Scourge of Corruption problem.

"Piranhas. Let's begin." Sheldon gestures to the large table. He says this every day.

There are twenty people in the room. On the walls, prints show reproductions of Piranha Frenzy's homepage down the years, from its 1990s origins as an old-school book company's web offshoot, through the blazing growth of the early '00s, right up to today, a twenty-year history of video games.

Sheldon has worked on many of these front pages, has been instrumental in their designs and tweaks over the years. They are his life's work.

He has spent his career fighting against competitors. First against the lumbering but powerful old magazine publishers, Future and Ziff. Then against Piranha Frenzy's bitter NorCal rivals IGN and GameSpot, the three of them forever trading the coveted traffic-numbers top slot. Now he fights against all the smart, targeted, ferociously keen blogs and start-ups as well as the social networks and game publisher shill-sites that nibble at his market share.

"Yeah, let's begin," says Brad, forcing a smile. "Awesome job yesterday, guys. We scored huge, huge numbers. With day six of the G2G preview and a retrospective on *Street Fighter IV*, as well as the rumor of a slim, pink PlayStation 4..."

Sheldon listens as Brad runs through the big wins of the last twenty-four hours. As always, the top five stories have taken 90% of the day's non-legacy traffic. The traffic-wins are celebrated. The stories that failed to spark are forgotten. Lessons about what people want to read, to view, to listen to, are digested.

Sheldon has already seen the numbers. He knows they are not enough to arrest Piranha Frenzy's continued traffic decline. Each year, for the past five years, they have lost at least a tenth of their readership. Each year, they lose out to Facebook, Twitter, Reddit, to smaller, more agile competitors, to snarky websites that taunt the old guard, to bloggers and YouTube playthroughs and e-sports destinations.

Sheldon is already tired of the soft stuff. "Let's move on to some of the more problematic issues, eh, Brad, old pal?"

Brad looks down at a printed agenda, emailed to him by Sheldon twenty minutes previously. "Yeah, uh, I thought the story about how RPGs in this generation are failing to, what was the headline? 'Why Do Today's RPGs Stink?' I thought that was questionable, and so we made some changes. Uh, Frank, we agreed that this sort of stuff is really not us."

Frank looks pretend-surprised by Brad's comment. "The treatment was valid," says Frank. "It's been at least two years since we saw a wholly original RPG. The decision to subsequently water the headline down to 'How Can RPGs Get Even Better?' was, in my view, unnecessary, questionable, you might say. I might use the word 'spineless' or perhaps 'craven.'"

Sheldon allows himself a smile.

"Yeah, I respect that," says Brad. "But how does your, kind of, aggressive stance help the reader? I mean, if you're an RPG fan, do you really want to hear about how bad they are today, which is just a point of view anyway?"

"That's why we flagged it as an opinion piece," says Frank, with a hint of acidity. "That it has a point-of-view is the entire, well, point."

"The article was inappropriate," says Steve Carter, interjecting physically, leaning far into the table. "It was the sort of snarky trash I'd expect to see in some reader forum garbage."

Sheldon says nothing. It was he who had instructed Brad to change the headline following a complaint from the advertising department, which in turn had been generated by a roar of disapproval from one of Piranha Frenzy's biggest advertisers, Saturnine.

"It just seems like we were being negative for the sake of it," says Brad. He waits for a response.

Frank shrugs.

This is Brad's function, thinks Sheldon. This is why I hired him. To make sure the stories hit their readership targets without annoying the sales team, to keep the editorial people in line, most especially Frank.

The old Australian has a different function, one he has decided upon without reference to the hierarchy. For Frank, this is a daily routine, pushing against Brad, arguing about stories, showing off his old-school, anti-establishment credentials to the young reporters.

Sheldon dislikes this little rebellion in principle, although it satisfies his desire to see Brad squirm from time to time, and so he allows it to continue, up to a point.

"I am the last line of defense against you fucking barbarians." A few months before, Frank had yelled this at Sheldon and some other execs, at a boozy Christmas party. It was a ludicrously overblown line. But Sheldon had seen nods from some on the editorial team, emboldened by a few too many ales. They had agreed with the sentiment.

Sheldon has snuffed out rebellions before. He decides it might be time to deal with Frank. He's been entertaining, but he's a problem that's been in need of resolution for months, maybe even years.

The meeting has moved onto an argument about a news story, some glitch that Sheldon has uncharacteristically missed. He chews his popcorn, waits to hear more.

"That story about the Japanese scientific submarine that happened to have the same name as a character in *Onimusha: Mercenary Sword,*" complains one of the new reporters, Zoe Zeller. "He's actually a real historical person too. He was an engineer in the early twentieth century. It just makes us look like morons."

Sheldon recalls the story. At the time, he'd thought it was just fluff, something lifted from Reddit: "Super Sub Named for Onimusha Warrior."

"That story did over 100,000 page views," Brad replies evenly. "Not bad."

"Because of a stupid, misleading headline," says Zoe. "Do you really think they named a submarine after a game character? It makes us look like we have no cultural horizons outside of games. Dumb."

In recent months, Sheldon has taken the hint from HR that more women ought to be hired onto the editorial team. Zeller is pretty much what he had expected all along, a troublesome minx with altogether too much to say for herself.

"Traffic-bait," says Charlie Black, from the back of the room. This interjection surprises Sheldon. Black rarely says a word.

"Wasn't it your story, Charlie?" asks Sheldon, turning toward the young reporter.

Charlie stares back, looks him in the eye. Another rarity. "No. I'm not a moron," he says.

"The reader response speaks for itself," says Steve Carter, leaning so far forward that Sheldon has to actually move his popcorn for fear it will tip over. "Surely you can see that."

This elicits a groan from the editors sitting around Frank at the other end of the room.

"Steve. You fucked up," Sheldon says. "You didn't check the story. Own it."

Steve stares back, his face reddens to within a few Pantone shades of his wiry hair. But after a moment, he bows his head and holds his hands up.

Zoe Zeller starts talking about some feature she's been pitching for months, without success. Sheldon watches Steve, wonders again if this erratic fellow really has the chops to one day be EIC.

He tunes back in to Zoe.

"...when we came into this generation it really seemed like the publishers understood that we'd moved on from the teenage boy masturbation days," she says.

Now it's the other end of the table that groans: Steve and his pals.

"Misogyny!" squeaks one in a fake-girly voice. Laughter. Sheldon turns and frowns at them. He feels it's his duty to bring some gravitas to the proceedings.

"I agree with Zoe," says Kjersti. "The marketing stuff has been getting worse. Some of this is really very unpleasant. Other outlets are addressing this issue while we stand by. It makes us look culpable."

"That's right," says Brad, jumping into a tiny pause in the conversation. "Other outlets are covering this and doing a great job. So let's leave them to it. What is the point of us weighing in as well?"

"The point, Brad, is that we have talented journalists who have valuable things to say about this issue," says Frank. "The point is that you're trying to muzzle them, because you're afraid these opinions will challenge the bias of many of our readers."

"Let the feminist blogs handle this," says Steve. "Our audience has made it clear this does not interest them. We seem to want to wish our audience is something that it isn't."

"You're just listening to a tiny, tiny proportion of our audience," says Kjersti. "The noisy trolls who we fear too much."

"Because their opinions just so happen to correlate with our policy of appeasing offensive marketing campaigns from big publishers," says Frank.

"Kjersti ought to talk to her lover directly about this, " says Steve. "If she is so keen to change the world of game advertising."

"That's enough," snaps Sheldon. He feels his temper rising. "We have more important issues to discuss. We are not covering this feature. That's the end of the matter. Let's move on."

The room is quiet for a moment. Kjersti glares at Steve, then goes back to making some notes, shaking her head.

"So most of you will be on your way to the Convention Center," says Brad. "Don't forget at G2G that you represent Piranha Frenzy and everything that we stand for, and with it being our twentieth birthday—woohoo, awesome—there'll be a big event on the main stage at 10 a.m. tomorrow which you are expected to attend. With that in mind, it's more important than ever that we conduct ourselves appropriately."

Sheldon notes an uncomfortable shuffling in seats, murmurs of disapproval at this patronizing lecture.

He decides to interject. "Most of you know how to work a convention," he says. "Those who have not done this before, take your lead from older hands. Any questions before we wrap up?"

Steve Carter raises his arm, crooked with a hanging index over his forehead. "What about this Scourge of Corruption thing? Any news?"

Brad begins to speak, but Sheldon holds his hand up to the EIC to indicate that he wishes to address the question and Brad's goatee stops moving, in mid-sentence, and his mouth closes.

"If anyone talks to you about this," Sheldon says, "tell them we have nothing to hide."

"The trouble with that," says Frank, "is that when this blogger—and I think we all know who he is—has run these stories in the past, a few years ago, granted, they have generally been extremely convincing."

"I'm just not comfortable saying that 'we' have nothing to hide, when that might not be, in fact, true," says Zoe.

Sheldon feels sure that junior writers, back in the day, kept their fucking mouths shut when it was time for the big boys to do the talking.

"We have nothing to hide," repeats Sheldon, speaking slowly, trying to control his voice. "But yes, it's prudent to wait and see what this blogger has to say and then, if necessary, launch an inquiry into whether or not we have a disgruntled leaker in our midst." He smiles, takes a handful of popcorn.

"Perhaps it might also be good," says Frank, "once we hear what this person has to say, to look into the actual corruption that is being alleged."

"Crazy idea," Zoe exclaims.

"Look. There is no corruption," says Sheldon, in a voice he hopes conveys patient self-assurance. "Just a lot of conspiracy theories. I'll keep you informed of any developments. Meantime, no need to start panicking. Now, are we finally done?"

"I have just one tiny thing. Kjersti," says Brad. "What do you think of *Satanic Realm 5*? Getting pretty close to deadline now."

"The review will be ready on time," she says, looking squarely at the EIC.

Sheldon shifts in his chair, swallows some popcorn, perhaps a tad underchewed. He feels fear bloom in his stomach, recognizes that the problem of the day is not some rancid blogger, but this woman and her review of the year's biggest game.

"I don't doubt it," says Sheldon. "But presumably, at this point in time you know what you think about it?"

"I do," she says. "As will everyone else, when the review runs."

There is a long silence. The room is waiting for Sheldon to demand to know the score, something the ethics guidelines clearly prohibit.

"I think I'd like to see copy before publication," says Sheldon. "Understood, Kjersti?"

"Absolutely understood," she says.

The meeting breaks up.

Frank is one of the last to pass Sheldon. The publisher leans out, slowly, blocking Frank's way with his arm.

"Have you got time, Frank, for a chat, about 3-ish? Just a few things to catch up on."

Frank looks surprised and alarmed. This pleases Sheldon.

4

A BROKEN PROMISE

11:49 a.m.

Kjersti heads out of the meeting, glad that it's finished. She's spent most of it thinking about *Satanic Realm 5*. She knows that all games, to some extent, build on the achievements on the past—"iterate" in the jargon of the designers—but this is way more specific.

In the corridor, a group of editors are gathering around a nest of arcade machines that have somehow accumulated over the years, an *Afterburner*, a *Defender*, a *Rampage*.

The only people who play them are visitors. But they're a focus for non-management to hang around after unhappy meetings, to exchange the words of rebellion that they don't have the courage to outright say to the bosses.

There's also a coffee machine. Kjersti waits in line.

Sheldon is heading toward her, patting Steve's shoulders. Kjersti fears the publisher is seeking some kind of rapprochement after the ugliness in the meeting, a ghastly shaking of hands.

She desperately wants to get back to her desk, so she can figure out this *Satanic Realm 5* problem. She'd spent most of the Morning Meeting writing down, rather too devotedly, a long list of games that might have been used as inspiration for the game, but nothing has provided a fit.

"I want you to come to my office," says Sheldon, beaming a smile that suggests bountiful munificence. He is an unusually fat man, dressed in a black outfit that gestures toward the respectability of a suit. Kjersti is glad that the popcorn has been left behind. It has become, for them all, the smell of dreary meetings, rather than of pleasant times in cinemas.

"Sure, Sheldon." She abandons her quest for caffeine and joins the two men, working their way across the floor toward Sheldon's office.

They thread their way through the advertising sales department's zigzag of desks. A few sales guys look up from their phone calls, without much interest. Rounding a corner of cubicles, where the accounts and HR people sit, they approach Sheldon's glass-walled office, mounted on a platform, a Death Star overlooking the Piranha Frenzy operation.

A young man is standing in the office, staring out. She vaguely recognizes him, thinks he might be a visiting PR man. No, that's not right. In a social semipanic she tries to place him as they enter the room.

It comes to her just as she shakes the young man's hand.

"Liam. Welcome. What brings you here?"

"Great to meet you at last, Kjersti. Huge, huge fan of your work."

Liam Sullivan runs an anarchic daily YouTube show out of his home in Detroit. She watches it regularly. It's a touch too nutty for her tastes but she can see its appeal, nonstop jokes, irreverent approach to gaming's shibboleths. Frank is forever going on about the show's "amazing voice."

"Liam has been tempted, nay, persuaded to come and work for us," says Sheldon.

"Which show will you be working on?" asks Steve, a guarded note in his voice.

"His own," says Sheldon, laughing. "No need to worry, Steve. We're not kicking you to the curb. Not yet anyway," he laughs. "He'll be working his own show. We bought the whole thing, moved him to sunny L.A."

"We kept it secret, somehow," says Liam. "It's being announced today."

Kjersti steals a look at Steve. He has been angling for more camera time. This is not good news for him.

A cloud forms in her mind. This is not good for me, either, she realizes.

"They've been telling me for months to be more like you, Liam," she says. "Now I can just let you be you, because, after all, you're the best man for that job."

Nervous laughter. Kjersti's show is sometimes lambasted, externally and internally, for being too serious, too straight. This is evidently not a problem for Liam. On his show, he is openly gay, provocatively flamboyant and merciless in his destruction of trolls who dare send him homophobic emails and video-posts.

She likes this part of his show the most, the way he has succeeded in reaching out beyond gaming's core of lad-fans, the newness of his approach.

She comprehends the underlying office politics. Liam is being lined up as her replacement, not Steve's. Her video presentation days are coming to an end.

Sheldon organizes fresh coffee, seats everyone around a small table in his office. Brad joins them, takes a seat, greets Liam warmly.

I am not as disappointed as I ought to be, she thinks. "I'm so pleased you've joined us. Really," she says. "Your show is just what we need here."

Brad agrees. Steve says nothing.

"What she means," says Sheldon, "is that we are way too straight, and have been for way too long."

"Ah," says Liam, smiling. "So I'm the token queer. Good to know. I'll be sure to spread the rainbow hues."

"If I wanted a token, uh, gay person," says Sheldon, "I'd surely be able to find one for less money than we paid you, Liam." Office-joke laughter.

"Some of our audience are not as enlightened as we are here," says Steve. "Just a word of friendly warning, It might get rough."

There's an awkward moment in which everyone takes a sudden interest in their cups of coffee.

"I'm sure you're right, Steve," says Liam. "We'll have some fun with that. Maybe we can work together, Steve, you, me and Kjersti, to knock around some new ideas."

"That sounds like a great idea," says Brad.

But the garrulous Liam has already moved on. "Talking of having fun, seems like news of my joining is going to be overshadowed some. I was just reading about this Scourge of Corruption thing."

"Nothing like a conspiracy to spice up the day," says Sheldon. He affects a comedic demeanor of paranoia. "But who are the conspirators?" And now the menacing autocrat. He clasps a fist in his hand. "We must root them out at all costs!"

Brad laughs and Liam smiles politely.

"But perhaps not so funny tonight, at our G2G opening party," says Kjersti. "Isn't that when the blog post is timed to hit?"

At moments like these, she enjoys channeling a slightly humorless timbre.

Sheldon waves the notion down. "Ideally, this wouldn't be happening, right? But it'll be fine. We must be doing something right or we wouldn't always be such a big target."

"I think people will focus on the positives," says Brad. "We're a target because we're successful, right? We must be doing something right."

"Well said," laughs Sheldon, patting Brad on the shoulder.

"I heard a rumor that the Scourge of Corruption is an old colleague of yours, Sheldon," says Kjersti. "An editorial guy from way back when?"

"Don Roby," says Brad.

"Do you know Don?" asks Sheldon, turning to Brad with slightly overdone curiosity. "I did not know that."

"Uh, no, not personally. Only by reputation."

"A Broken Promise," says Kjersti, referring to Roby's notorious 1999 book. "I read it while I was at university."

"Well, well," says Sheldon, as if he is being reminded of some delightful old pal. "I haven't heard that name in an age." Kjersti recalls that Sheldon is featured in the book, a now outdated history of game journalism, in broadly unflattering terms.

"But blogging in secret was never his style," says Sheldon. "He likes the limelight too much. Alas, he doesn't see much of it. Last I heard he was living in some tiny Missouri town, a sub-editor for a local rag. He's moved on, and so has the rest of the world."

"The early Internet. Lots of back-biting and double-deals," says Liam.

"Life in the 1990s," Kjersti adds, sighing theatrically. "How different it was then."

Liam smiles broadly at her. We are going to be friends, she thinks.

"Crazy times," says Brad, missing her jab. "Wild West."

Sheldon is looking less happy with the conversation. "It was, as they say, a different time. Don, like a lot of guys, fell by the wayside. He coped with his disappointment by writing that book, and no one held it against him. It wasn't exactly a bestseller. A lot of what he said was right on the money, but some of it..." Sheldon looks regretful, as if the grisly exposé of Piranha Frenzy's earlier years had disappointed his own lofty ideals.

"Anyway, we're here for the future. And the future is you guys. Now, to business. Kjersti, seriously, how the hell is *Satanic Realm 5*?" He smiles at his own joke. "I didn't mean to press you in the meeting. It's just, we're all busy today; it's something on my to-do list."

She knows she's got to face it, she has to get away, do the research, find a quiet place and decide what she's going to write about this game. She's been avoiding the inevitable.

"Just about ready to write it up now," she says. "Better get a move on, I suppose." She stands, twists her wrists and lets her fingers mimic rapid typing, smiles, turns.

"Don't forget," Sheldon calls after her. "You need to get with Liam and organize schedules for presenting the G2G live-show. I want him getting equal airtime with you and Steve."

"Make sure I see that *Satanic Realm 5* copy before it goes live," yells Brad.

5

ROTTEN CORRUPTION

12:12 p.m.

Sitting at a broken, lopsided desk in the dark, deserted loft of Piranha Frenzy's office building, Charlie Black is eating a chicken salad sandwich and listening intently to his headphones, which are plugged into a laptop. He's tuned into a meeting between Brad Hoffman and Sheldon Tavernier happening a few floors beneath him.

In his headphones, Charlie hears Sheldon bitching about the editorial meeting, speaking derisively about Frank and Zoe. None of this really interests Charlie. He waits.

There is a lull in the conversation. He hears Sheldon let out a long sigh and then a ripping fart.

"Woah. I needed that."

"Nice," says Brad. "Shall I put that in the minutes?"

"No less articulate than some of the garbage we had to listen to this morning."

Charlie finishes his sandwich and waits. He is making a film, and he reckons it's a doozy.

A few months before, on the day Charlie bugged Piranha Frenzy's meeting rooms, he'd disguised himself as an electrician: fake beard, glasses, the works.

Of course, he could have bugged the rooms as Charlie Black, but that would not have been nearly so much fun, and it would have made far less of a visual treat in his film.

An audio device had been planted in the Small Meeting Room where he knows the bosses like to plot, and where they hold meetings with clients.

A video camera and audio pick-up had also been placed in the Big Meeting Room. There's so much junk in those rooms, it was easy.

He'd printed out business cards for the company Piranha Frenzy regularly used to handle its service maintenance work and made sure the installations were made on a day the office manager was away.

He'd even walked past a few colleagues, including Zoe and Steve, intensely enjoying the experience. But none of them had even looked at him.

Since then, he has been gathering footage of the film's main characters, Sheldon, Brad, a few others. He'd even thrown a party at his apartment, just to get some extra footage of them standing around drinking. And because he'd wanted them to know where he lives.

Now he's adding the finishing touches to the film. By his own estimates, 'The Rotten Corruption at the Heart of Video Game Reviews' will clock up ten million views on YouTube.

He has everything he really needs, but he wants to get some reactions from Brad and Sheldon on the news that they're about to be exposed by the Scourge. This is why he has dropped the note that a blog post is coming.

"So," says Brad. "The Scourge of Corruption. Your old friend Don Roby."

Now Charlie is alert.

"Yeah, it's him. Jesus. The guy just has zero life. Imagine spending your time writing about a company you left fifteen years ago."

"Strictly speaking, he didn't leave though."

"Well, no, he was fired for being a loser. A real man might have bought an M16 and come back to the office and gunned us all down, but, oh no, Don Roby has to blog like a…"

"Loser?" suggests Brad.

Charlie likes the line about the M16. Spectacularly poorly judged. Typical of Sheldon, to reach for an inappropriate image.

He listens as someone, probably Sheldon, takes a noisy sip of a drink.

"So, the problem is, who is the mole? And how do we discredit whatever BS this blog post has to offer?"

"If there is a mole," says Brad, "he or she must be on the editorial floor, or maybe the video department. And if that's true, we should maybe consider the possibility that he or she has got something potentially very damaging."

"But what could it be, really? We write about video games for chrissakes." Sheldon groans. "Fuck it. I need to take a shit. Back in a few."

Charlie listens to the noise of Sheldon getting out of his chair and leaving the room. He thinks about using this exchange over the credits at the end of the film.

The centerpiece of the film is a conversation that took place in The Big Meeting Room six weeks previously. It hadn't been the smoking gun that Charlie had hoped for, but it was more than enough to discredit his employer, especially when added together with all the other snippets and evidence he'd amassed.

Brad, Sheldon and Alejandro Bernal, not only chief marketing officer of Saturnine but also Kjersti Wong's glamorous fella, had been talking, bandying around BS phrases like "strategic cooperation" and "consumer alignment." Then they'd said a few words that gave Black all the ammunition he needed.

The words that had come out of their mouths, in a film, or quoted on the forums, would go down very badly. It helped that Brad had been spectacularly sleazy in his unctuous sucking up to Bernal.

Charlie knew this was enough. His dad, on viewing the video from their home back in Missouri, had agreed. The film was to be built around that meeting. They would complete it in time for Piranha Frenzy's twentieth birthday celebrations at G2G.

It would be the culmination of a five-year plot to infiltrate a leading game news website—preferably Dad's old employer Piranha Frenzy—and expose its corrupt inner workings.

Using his new nom de guerre, Charlie—real name Lars Roby—had launched a game blog, with behind-the-scenes secret help from his experienced father. It was a good blog. They'd worked hard and been rewarded with a growing audience.

Charlie repeatedly attempted to gain an internship at a big game website. Every failure had increased the pressure to succeed. His father had grown impatient. But eventually, on the back of the blog, he'd been accepted at Piranha Frenzy.

Bingo.

Taught relentlessly by his father to turn in crisp copy, on time, he had proven himself far superior to other interns, and had been offered a job as a news writer. For the first six months he'd kept his head down, worked hard, just jotted down surreptitious notes of damaging things said in meetings or on the editorial floor.

This was when the idea had come to him to make a film, rather than simply writing a blog or a book. He'd learned how to shoot secret footage, how to record meetings, how to hack into sensitive shared documents, how to create animations. He had enjoyed himself immensely. The six-minute film was almost complete.

As a side-quest, Charlie had more recently begun to plant entirely fictitious stories on the site. Brad, in his desire to hit traffic targets, would wave anything through on the flimsiest evidence, overriding Frank's objections time after time. All he had to do was couch the fake stories with weasel words like "reports are surfacing" or "sources allege that," and the bosses were happy. It was easy.

Charlie hears Sheldon return to the office, the door closing behind him.

"Suspects one and two," Sheldon says, groaning as he sits. "Frank and Zoe."

"Well, I don't..."

"Completely negative people. Always complaining."

"Maybe we should talk to them?" says Brad, uncertainly.

"Hm. I have a better idea. Let's discuss it over lunch."

"Lunch?" says Brad. Charlie can hear the fear in the man's voice. "I have tons of stuff to do, you know?"

"Rearrange it, man. Your boss is asking you out for lunch. Accept."

"OK. Lunch it is." Brad sounds glum.

"Well, now I have a meeting with our illustrious advertising manager. I hope that ass-eruption of mine has dissipated. Wouldn't want to offend the woman's delicate olfactory systems."

"No," agrees Brad. "It all seems, uh, clear now."

Brad quits the room. Charlie picks up his laptop. He wants to get back to the office. He can listen to this ad manager meeting later. In the meantime, he has a problem.

For one planned section of the movie, yet to be filmed, he needs Sheldon and Brad to suspect Charlie Black of being the mole. He has to get himself right to the top of Sheldon's list of suspects so he can capture them finally figuring it out.

He won't tell his father about this, Charlie decides. The old man might think it's too risky. He might say one of his regular lines like, "We're real close now, kid. Don't fuck this up."

This is my film, after all, thinks Charlie.

6

DORITOS

1:40 p.m.

Kjersti is starting to panic. She's spent too much time digging through old articles, trying to make a connection between *Satanic Realm 5* and whatever the hell is itching her memory. The embargo is only a few hours away.

She knows she ought to be writing the review. Instead, she's hanging around in the video editors' room, a soundproof glass booth attached to the recording studio, quietly editing today's edition of her show.

From her editing console she can see Steve Carter on the studio floor. Liam's there as well, with Angie, the tall, fierce producer. They are all prepping a new shoot.

Kjersti edits lightly, skips through the footage of herself rolling through some of the day's headlines. All it requires is a drop of pre-prepped B-Roll here and there. On screen she is interviewing Liam, the new guy, asking him a couple of softball questions. While she sticks to the script, he ad-libs. He's funny and natural.

Frank enters the booth, surprising her. He's hardly ever seen in the studio. "Can't you find some other Muppet to do that?" he says. "I know you've got better things to be doing."

"I know," says Kjersti. "This won't take long. Then I'll write it."

He sits down, and takes a long look at her.

"Something's wrong, Kjersti. You look completely frazzled."

She stops editing. "I just don't know what to say. I mean, I know there's something wrong. It's bugging me. I just can't nail it."

"How long does it take you to write a thousand words?"

"Maybe an hour."

"Then you have plenty of time. Just find a quiet place, empty your mind and get me that fucking copy."

She laughs.

They look out at the studio activity. "What do you make of Liam?" she asks him.

"He's just what we need, I think."

"He lives for this stuff. He's a natural. I think I'm finished."

They sit quietly for a few minutes; she turns back to the video edit. It's rote: the show, the script, the edit. It's the same every day.

"It's OK to move on, you know," says Frank. "It's OK to change who and what you are."

"You did it, Frank."

He gestures out to the studio floor. "They don't want you to change. They just want to make use of you, and when they're done..." He makes the poooof gesture.

"Honestly? Given a choice, I'd be happy to abandon video forever, to just sit and write about games, to focus..." She gestures at herself on screen. "I'm sick of this person."

She wants to say she is tired to her very teeth of flirty, self-mocking, nerd-ironic Kjersti and "Oh" and her fan mail and the gifts and the stupid, sad video messages she receives from desperately lonely and incredibly angry people.

Laughter spills into the editing suite. Liam is bantering to the camera. The teleprompter sits mute. On the editing console, a monitor flickers to life, carrying the camera feed.

"Yeah, you heard right," says Liam, speaking to camera. "I sold out to the man. I sold out to the evil Piranha Frenzy. So? What of it?"

"Here we go," says Frank, smiling like a proud schoolteacher.

Kjersti is going through the motions of editing her show. She drops in the standing credits, files the show as ready for publication.

"I'll let you into a little secret," says Liam. "It's a fiendish plot, to destroy the bad guys from the inside out. That and getting a way better wardrobe. So listen, do please leave your comments because I read them all, or at least the ones by people who make correct use of apostrophes and have figured out how to spell 'faggot.' Two Gs, people."

Kjersti looks at Frank. He's grinning, enjoying the show.

"In the meantime, I want to assure each and every one of my fans and admirers that I'll always be the same fearless reporter who absolutely refuses to kowtow to corporate interests."

At this, he starts drinking from a Big Gulp cup of 7Up, lasciviously pouring the liquid over his face. He starts eating, messily, from a bag of Doritos, pours those over his face. It's an old joke, but it gets a laugh from the crew.

Kjersti and Frank both laugh. "You know," says Frank. "Before he started doing his show, he was making how-to videos for $10 a throw?"

In the darkness behind camera, she sees Steve Carter, typing something into a tablet. Liam cleans up after himself and then quits the floor.

"Steve, you're on now," says Angie. "Have you got the script?"

"Emailing it now to teleprompter," he yells.

Kjersti really needs to write that review, but still, she cannot push beyond the weight of consequences, cannot decide what she is going to say about a game that she dislikes, without being entirely certain why.

"Have you seen those early how-to videos?" she asks Frank. He shakes his head. "I should search for them, see how much it's inherent, how much he's bolted on over the years."

"Not much time for this, Steve," says Angie. "It's just a short, friendly welcome to Liam to post on the website and link to his YouTube hub. Keep it simple. Let Liam do the jokes, OK?"

Steve nods, but doesn't look happy. He steps up to the mark and his face transforms to a wonky smile.

Kjesti thinks again about *Satanic Realm 5*, about the franchise's twenty-year evolution, how much it has changed since that first game, so well known, so familiar, the subject of countless nostalgic YouTube walkthroughs. She thinks of her time playing games with her father, of his boxes of disks and cassettes. Then she remembers, clearly. It comes to her almost like a feeling, a being back there, back then, with her father. With the memory of him, she finds the puzzle's answer.

Steve delivers his monologue to camera. "From the bulging bottom of our hearts, here at Piranha Frenzy, we want to offer a squealingly excited welcome to our flamboyant new host, luscious Liam Sullivan. Can't wait to give him sweaty no-homo hugs. We mere mortals are not worthy to lick the glistening man-sweat from the underside of his sweet testicles. So if you want the whole shaft of his thrusting wit, stay tuned."

These last two words are delivered in a grotesque parody of an effeminate man.

There's a moment's silence in the studio.

"What a fool that lad is," says Frank.

"That was unfunny and wrong," shouts Angie. "Seriously, Steve. We don't have time for this. Let's just kill it."

Liam steps out. "It's OK. It's fine. It didn't work, Steve, but I think I appreciate what you were trying to do."

"I think we all do," says Angie, still furious.

Kjersti watches, but her mind is reaching now, back in time, further back than she had previously thought.

"What the fuck is wrong with you people," says Steve. He stands, arms outstretched, beseeching the camera lights. "I don't think you have the first clue about our audience."

Kjersti glances at the screens on the editing suite. The unfolding studio scene is still running on one of them, Steve, plum on his mark.

"This isn't the '90s," says Angie. "In the future, all of your scripts are to be submitted to me well in advance."

"OK, I get it." Steve is yelling now. "Mustn't offend anyone. Mustn't make any jokes that might spoil someone's day. I mean, we can have a gay guy doing the queer jokes, but not a straight guy? It's... fuck this PC bullshit." He stalks off.

The screen blinks blank and reverts to a file list. Kjersti sits and looks at it for a long moment. Members of the studio floor crew are standing around, waiting for Angie's word.

"This mustn't stand," says Frank.

Kjersti reaches into a pencil box and pulls out an ancient memory card, tartan-sleeved.

Frank's eyes widen.

She doesn't think of herself as a schemer, has never gone in for leaking information or bad-mouthing colleagues. But she wants to do this, without knowing why.

"Holy shit," whispers Frank. "Holy shit, Kjersti."

She slots the stick onto a USB slot on the console, copies the file across.

"OK. That was fun," says Angie. "Let's get the rest of this gear down to the convention center. It's G2G time. All lives are hereby suspended until further notice."

"Jesus, Kjersti. What are you going to do?" asks Frank.

She puts the USB stick in her jeans pocket. "I've figured it out. I'm going to write that review."

7

THE WHITEBOARD

2:12 p.m.

Charlie has managed to make zero progress in his plan to place himself under Brad and Sheldon's suspicion as the Piranha Frenzy mole.

The bosses have been in meetings for the last few hours. There's no sign of Kjersti. Zoe already told him to get lost once today, when he sidled up to her desk and tried to interrupt her writing a feature. She'd called him a creep.

Frank is still sulking because he, Charlie, managed to persuade Brad to agree to a bogus story headlined "Source: Nintendo Considering New F-Zero." Charlie slipped a fake Pilotwings rumor into the lede, just for kicks.

His best chance, he believes, is in the weekly Features Meeting taking place in the Small Meeting Room.

He knows Brad will be there and so will Frank, and in the sparks that are bound to fly between these two, he can generate illumination.

When Charlie arrives, there are only three other journos attending, as well as Brad and Frank. Kjersti, who rarely misses a meeting, is absent, heads down with her perilously deadline-skirting *Satanic Realm 5* review. Zoe is still working on her feature.

Brad is standing at a whiteboard writing down a list of feature ideas, which Charlie makes a point of inspecting at close quarters.

FEATURE IDEAS!!!
GTA's Most Badass Villains
If Game Characters Were Celebs
Mashed Up: Mario and Maribelle
Ten Facts About Assassin's Creed: The Boxer Rebellion
Why We Love Borderlands
Ten Best Game Console Designs Ever
What We Want From Civ 6

Charlie snorts derisively at the list, finds a spot against the wall to stand. He affects a pose of scornful semi-attendance, fiddles with a 2DS.

"This is fucking drivel," says Frank, smiling easily. "Bland pap. The same mindless shit, day in and day out."

Charlie is gratified that his predictions of feature-related strife have proven so prescient.

"Well, Frank," says Brad evenly. "Maybe you have some better ideas?"

"OK, Brad, let's start, as you have, obviously, with Grand Theft Auto." Frank stands up, pushes his chair away. "How about 'GTA Is Reductive, Derivative, Misogynistic White-Boy, Middle-Class Fantasy Trash.'"

"Well, that's an interesting opin..."

"Talking of Assassin's Creed, how about, 'Has any entertainment form ever done a worse job with historical fiction than video games?'"

"That's just not relev..."

"Seeing as we're not allowed to write any words that question gaming's disgusting sexism, maybe we can persuade some top female artists to redesign iconic female game characters, or rework some of the most egregious cover art."

"That seems very expens..."

"How about, 'Why game consoles are a gross intrusion on your privacy.' Imagine the traffic, Brad. Imagine the social shares."

"We're not here to merely generate traffic."

Charlie grins as the junior journos in the room squirm. He's glad that this meeting is being recorded. Maybe he can make a sequel to his film. He can make a great deal of money out of these films.

"It's all pointless, of course, Brad," says Frank. "The brain-dead features you have placed on the whiteboard are the ones that will be waved through, will make their inexorable way onto our front page in the weeks to come, and will be converted into page views and thence to ad hits and to revenues."

"That's what pays our wages, after all, Frank," says Brad. "I gotta say, the way you are speaking to me is not cool. Not cool at all."

"You asked me for ideas. I gave you them. I think they're... awesome."

Frank laughs and holds his hands out, seeking approval from the group. The journos scowl at him, all except Charlie who is now softly chortling to himself.

Charlie thinks of how much his father would enjoy this meeting, how angry he is, in fact, that he is not here. Dad's golden career in game journalism was stunted by what the old man always calls "Sheldon Tavernier and the Spineless Sell-Out Crew," as if they were some cheesy rap band from the early '80s.

"I have an opinion on this," says Charlie, breaking the awkward silence.

Everyone turns toward him. This is his chance.

"News is just stuff that happens. Reviews and previews are all based on PR schedules. Features is the only place where we can just say what we want.

"It seems a shame to waste that by just rehashing the same stuff over and over again. It makes us look like shills, so it's not surprising that we have employees who are leaking to hostile bloggers."

Frank's face is one huge grin. He begins clapping.

"Bravo, that fella. I don't know who he is, but he looks a lot like our impish news writer Charlie Black, except with a curious ability to talk sense. Who knew he had it in him, eh, Brad?"

Charlie hopes this little speech has put him in the frame as a possible disenfranchised editorial grunt, leaking secrets to the bogeyman.

"I had no idea you thought this way, Charlie," says Brad, as if he were talking to a child who questions the existence of divinities. "You know, we're always open to conversations, criticisms—that's how we progress."

"Progress. That's right," says Charlie. "Maybe this Scourge of Corruption guy is doing us a favor. Progress is always painful, right?"

Frank looks back at Brad. Brad looks at Charlie. The other journos look anywhere they can.

"Well, this has been fascinating," says Brad, finally. "Amazing exchange of views. Unfortunately, with G2G, well, time is running out, so let's wrap it up and get back to work and maybe..."

Brad drones on. Charlie is thinking about his film, thinking about how this is his last day working for Piranha Frenzy, his last day, almost certainly, writing about video games for a living. The meeting breaks up.

He is still in the room, after everyone has left, after Frank has touched his shoulder on the way out and said, "Well done, mate."

His cell phone is in his hand, his thumb and finger hover, ready to send a text to his dad, one of the dozens of reports that he sends home every day. His fingers pause over the touchscreen. He puts the phone in his pocket.

8

NOBLE FLESH

3:10 p.m.

Sheldon orders the two biggest steaks in the kitchen, a side of fries and a Coke. Brad earns a look of contempt from his boss when he orders a Greek salad and a glass of water.

"Thou shalt consume the noble flesh," says Sheldon, holding his hands up in monkish pose. "In order that thou will survive the perils ahead." He dips a French roll into a bowl of olive oil.

Brad smiles weakly, and this reassures Sheldon that his subordinate is suitably worried about the meeting. The sunglasses have been stowed away, Sheldon notices. Brad's eyes are small and pale.

It has been Sheldon's habit, for some years, to fire his unwanted EICs at lunch meetings. He finds public spaces more convenient for getting rid of senior staff, once they have outlasted their usefulness. It is always interesting to see how people react when they are given bad news in public.

In the decade since he held the position himself, Sheldon has fired eight EICs. Usually the news has come as a surprise to his victims.

This one though, Brad, will not be fired today. He is proving much too useful as a willing gofer. An EIC who just does what he is told, without endless inconvenient questions and caveats, is a rare thing.

"OK," says Sheldon. "Down to business. Let's talk about *Satanic Realm 5*."

Brad looks troubled. "I asked for the copy on my desk at 12, but still nothing." He checks his phone, in vain it turns out, for an incoming email from Kjersti.

Sheldon enjoys Brad's use of the phrase "on my desk," the proprietorial sense of ownership, the illusion of permanence and control it suggests.

But he does not enjoy the discomfort of knowing that he will be meeting with Saturnine's marketing boss Alejandro Bernal in a few hours, to discuss budgets for the year ahead, coupled with the possibility, however remote, that the encounter will be rendered unproductive by a less-than-glowing review of one of the year's biggest games.

"Forget the copy," he says. "What I want to know is the score. Just the number."

"Kjersti is being mysterious."

"I don't get it," says Sheldon. "She loves this series. She gave *Satanic Realm 4* an 85%. She's dating the guy who is marketing the damned thing. What is she waiting for?"

The drinks arrive. Sheldon takes his time enjoying a slurp of Coke.

"You know how she is," says Brad.

"Not really, Brad. No. I don't know how she is, nor do I give a fuck. What I do know is that if the score is going to be higher than, say, 83, we could have made Saturnine's ad buyers aware of this happy fact 24 hours ago..."

"Sure, sure," says Brad, nodding, looking down at his napkin.

"And they would have given us at least a few hours exclusive on one of the biggest articles of the year, yielding some much-needed traffic, the very thing that you, Brad, are paid to produce. Right now, we would be splashing merrily in a running river of traffic and I would be festooning you with 'ataboys.' But that hasn't happened."

"Kjersti," says Brad, making a slight movement of his hands, indicating frustration, "she is one of those who doesn't believe in exclusives and refuses to give out her score before copy submission. She says it leads to corrupt practices and in this, perhaps, she has a poi..."

"Her score?" hisses Sheldon. He feels a familiar rage against these precious scribblers. "She does not own the review. I do... I mean... Piranha Frenzy does. We need to know what the score is, well in advance, so we can monetize it as effectively as possible. I am sure I have already asked you to get a grip on this, Brad. This is the way we do business, and it is not Kjersti Wong's job to frustrate our process."

"Yes, but, I think, the tide is turning against this—the readers are very suspicious of exclusives."

The food arrives. Brad moves cutlery and his glass to make room for the plates. He glances up, and looks afraid.

"A few losers on the forums may have a problem with the way the world turns," says Sheldon, slicing into one of his steaks. "But they are not our concern. They do not number the million or so people who will read this review in the next twenty-four hours, or the million or so extra people who would have read it, had we stolen a march on our rivals, but who will instead read it on RPS or Polygon or Eurogamer."

He glares at Brad, chewing furiously. "I am not going to sit by and watch us lose readers, and money, because of a few whining bitches on Twitter."

"Yes, yes, of course, it's a business. I understand."

"And none of this answers my question, which is, what is the review score that we are giving, in a few hours time, to *Satanic Realm 5*?"

Brad plays with his Greek salad.

Sheldon has a memory of a fantasy novel he enjoyed a few years back, in which the dead exist in a place of nothingness, a gloom of despair that offers a constant, painful glimpse of the joy of living. By some power, they are allowed to escape, back to the world of the living, away from the suffering of nonexistence.

This, in Sheldon's view, is Brad's career. He was an unspectacular reviewer for a range of moderately successful outlets before being loosed into the void by one of the sweeping plagues of layoffs that regularly descend upon game journalism. He had then taken some miserable job as a community manager on an MMO. And there he had floated, for years, disconnected from the thrumming vibrations of journalism, dealing with the horror of PR people as demanding superiors rather than as grinning supplicants, dealing with consumers as righteous customers rather than as readers and fans.

Sheldon saved Brad from this purgatory. Fresh from firing the last EIC, who'd suffered from the delusion that Piranha Frenzy required "improvements," Sheldon had been in the market for someone with the quality he most required: acquiescence.

And boy, had Brad delivered. The poor fool lived in a state of constant terror that he might, at any stage, be sucked back into the void. Community management and the non-career that followed was a mere flick of a finger away. They both knew it.

Satisfied that there will be no answer to his question, Sheldon continues with his lunch.

"I like you, Brad," he says. "We agree on how Piranha Frenzy needs to be run. But you have a weakness, and that weakness is your timidity in the face of your team. I did not hire you to be liked by them, I did not hire you to be scared of them. I hired you to get them to do the things that require doing."

"I know, Sheldon. I know, bu…"

"We are not making as much money as we need to be making. We are losing audience. There is too much at stake here." He stops for a moment, regards the piece of meat on the end of his fork, and waves it at Brad. "Steak. Geddit?"

Brad smiles, seems to appreciate the opportunity to speak.

"I take your point. I really do. I'll work on it. But as far as *Satanic Realm 5* goes, we haven't actually made any guarantees to Alejandro. We were clear to him. Church and state. No guarantees. That would be wrong."

"That would be wrong," nods Sheldon, speaking very quietly, a wave of pure rage sweeping through him, as he swallows a slightly-too-large chunk of beef.

"Are you a fucking moron, Brad?" He feels the anger biting, remembers what he has been taught about self-control.

"I'm sorry to be blunt," he says. "Alejandro agreed to spend $1.5 million of Saturnine's money, advertising on our site between now and the end of the year, with a further $1 million up for grabs in a meeting to be held...," Sheldon theatrically regards his watch, "in a few hours' time."

Brad tries to interject, but Sheldon holds his hand up.

"You can see why I am upset. There were certain expectations agreed upon, unspoken agreements that a man of common sense would understand."

"That's not how I recall..."

"This is the money that is going to keep me and you, Brad, in work for the rest of the year. We made no guarantees because it would be wrong to do so, but also because there is no need to do so. *Satanic Realm 5* is a stand-up game that many people will enjoy very much. It merits a good score. But now I begin to worry that Kjersti might be deciding, in her boundless wisdom, to not give it a good score.

"And so, talking of things that are wrong, I worry that you made the wrong decision in giving this game to her to review, when you could just as easily have done it yourself, understanding, as I'm sure you do, the sensitivities here."

Brad nods. He is pale now. "She seemed so right for it," he said. "Yes. I made a mistake. I've been super busy. I should have just handled this. But, she reviewed last year's game and she liked it and she insisted. As you say, there's the thing with Alejandro and her, which has got to be worth a few percentage points. Maybe... she's always a bit secretive about her reviews, even when they are positive. I don't think we need to worry too much she..."

"You're babbling now, Brad," says Sheldon. "Calm down. Eat your salad."

Sheldon takes some comfort in the probability, as he sees it, that Kjersti is just playing out, and will score the game at 85% or above.

"We have been doing this a long time now," he says, feeling a calmness return. "One of the reasons we're still here, why we're still on top, is because we keep doing the stuff that people like, the stuff that they want, and, as far as possible, we don't change that. The delivery might have changed, more videos, more wikis, whatever, but the format stays the same. You like games. We like games. Buy more games. Everyone is happy."

Brad does not look happy. "That seems like a slightly cynical view," he says.

Sheldon wonders, for a moment, if he has gone too far, if he has once again said too much. Always he is wary of the unguarded comment finding its way into the public domain. He thinks, as he has every day for the past sixteen years, of A Broken Promise, of how he had been portrayed so negatively, as a bounder, how he was betrayed by Don Roby.

"You're right," he says, mollifying. "It's too much. I just mean that consistency is important. So, let's change the subject to trying to figure out who our mole is."

And so they drift into yet another conversation about who on the team might be giving away secrets. They begin bandying names around.

"What about Charlie?" says Brad. "He seemed discontented in the features meeting today, and was even praising The Scourge."

"Too young. Too eager. Too invested in the greasy pole. I mean, he even threw a house party. Remember?" But Sheldon notes this: It's not as if anyone really trusts

Charlie Black.

"I suppose he's kinda the opposite of Frank," says Brad. "And yet, I sense him picking up some of Frank's bad habits, like Kjersti..."

Sheldon chews on the last of his steak, pops a few fries in his mouth. Brad looks as if he wants to bite back the word "Kjersti," the dangerous implication that she has gone rogue, that she might now be hard to predict, that the review score might not be as anticipated.

"Hmmmm. Hmmmmm," chews Sheldon. He notes Brad's clumsy allusion, but he has other issues to deal with now. "It's curious that you should mention Frank."

"Why?"

"It's time for good old Frank to go."

Sheldon watches Brad for a reaction and notices that he does not seem too distressed by the news that he is losing a team member.

"Why Frank?"

"We need to make cuts more than we need a copy editor," explains Sheldon. "In any case, Frank is obviously not happy. He's always picking fights. He's a negative influence. Come on, Brad, it's not like you and he are friends."

"No," says Brad. "But he is popular. And he is competent. I assume we're doing this after G2G?"

"No. We're doing it today. Get it out of the way."

Unhappily, Brad looks at the remainder of his salad. "And who will edit the copy now?"

"That," says Sheldon, waving his fork at Brad, "is your problem."

9

UNDER EMBARGO

3:38 p.m.

At the coffee shop across from Piranha Frenzy's offices, Alejandro is sitting down with an elegant little espresso in front of him, taking a phone call. On the table sits a giant frothy latte, her regular.

He is wearing a fashionably cut suit, an understated tie, knotted exactly according to the glossy magazine mores. When she enters the shop, he cuts his phone conversation short, smiles and stands.

He smiles often. With her, he is kind, generous and attentive. He is funny and clever. He is the best-connected man in the video game business. He is a man of charm, well-liked, someone who shares her love of games, who knows the business inside and out.

"You OK?" he asks before kissing her.

"I needed to get out of the office. It's crazy in there today."

He looks at his watch. She wonders if he is thinking about the review embargo.

"You work too hard." He gives her a look of concern.

He kisses her again and they sit. She gulps the coffee.

"If we're pictured here, and then the review posts, it will cause a media scandal," he says, smiling.

"Only if the review is positive."

"Which I am confident it will be. I take it you got it finished?"

"I suppose this little picture of us together would make another Alejandro-and-Kjersti meme," she jokes, ignoring his question. She knows he enjoys his geek-celebrity status.

Alejandro Bernal is a familiar figure on r/gaming and NeoGAF. His publicity shots have been doctored in a million ways, often disparagingly referring to some evil new DRM policy from Saturnine; policies which, she knows, he despises.

They have this in common, the pleasures and burdens of inconsequential, fleeting niche celebrity.

The fanboys accuse him of the alleged dumbing down of beloved franchises, or refusing to resurrect old games, or pandering to the mainstream. He personifies Evil Game Corporation, although she finds his views on these matters complex and thoughtful. There are few people more critical of Saturnine than Alejandro Bernal, although, in public, he dutifully mouths the company's lines.

Three months before, when they'd begun dating in public, photographs of the two of them having dinner together at a fancy restaurant had been posted online. It had generated a game-media uproar. They'd trended on Twitter.

If gaming could be said to have a glamour couple, Kjersti and Alejandro were it.

Over their coffees, they make small talk about his day, about G2G. He avoids mentioning *Satanic Realm 5* again, even though it's the company's big play for the summer and obviously dominating his time completely.

She watches him and his easy grace. He is not like her previous partners who have been, generally, bohemian, awkward, poor and obscure. Not for the first time, she wonders if he represents a sort of vacation for her, a break from all those relationships in which she was forced to be the grown-up. Or perhaps, this is how relationships ought to work; without grinding labor or too much in the way of fuss and bother.

Time with him is also a vacation from all the other men, her colleagues at work. The hostility of Steve and his like; Sheldon and Brad and their faintly dismissive distance. Even Frank, his bluff, fatherly patois that veers into patronizing territory, despite his own best efforts to master deeply embedded behavior patterns. She is always, with them, somehow in combat mode.

They chat about small things until, finally, she changes the subject. She wants his advice. "There's this thing, and I don't know what to do about it," she says. "Steve Carter, in the office, going too far."

While she was writing the review, she'd uploaded the file to her phone. She plays it for him.

"What a dick," he says, frowning, touching his fingers together.

"There's a blog coming out from the Scourge of Corruption. Now this. Rebellion is in the air. The meeting this morning, the atmosphere was poisonous. It's really bad there right now."

"I've told you before to get out of there. Do your own thing. You're too big for them."

"I wish you'd said I was too good for them."

"That too..." he pauses. For a moment he seems to stop, to recalibrate. There is always this too, with him, the sense of performance. "Are you planning to leak this?"

"I don't know. It might hurt Steve. It might hurt Piranha Frenzy. It might hurt me."

"Nonsense," he laughs. "The world needs to see this moron as he really is." She suspects he's enjoying the possibility of intrigue.

He shakes his head. Like many people who work in gaming, Alejandro holds a poor opinion of game journalists. "My God," he says. "This ass-hat is next in line to be EIC of one of the biggest news outlets in the industry. It's a joke. Piranha Frenzy are such a bunch of idiots."

She nods. Sips the last of her latte. She wants to ask him about *Satanic Realm 5*, about her suspicions, but what good would it do now? The review is done, she thinks. She's afraid to ask. She's afraid of being wrong, of being told she is wrong.

"Quit that place. I keep telling you, Kjersti."

She has heard this many times. Sometimes they argue. She waves it away.

"Send the file to me," he says, gesturing with his hand. "I know someone who can make a quick edit, post it completely anonymously and be sure it's seen by lots of people."

"More of your black ops marketing ninjas?" she says. "I don't know. It seems..."

"Machiavellian. Sneaky? Yeah, Kjersti. But this dude is a nasty bastard. He's been spouting low-level hate for years."

"We're not exactly being noble here. Is this... personal ambition or personal dislike? Either way, it feels wrong."

"You took the file for a reason," he says. "We're letting Carter damn himself, with his own words." He shrugs and says, "I listened to his show this morning. He tried to throw you under the bus."

She pulls the tartan memory stick from a pocket, studies it, looks at him. "I guess I just don't like what he stands for," she says and hands it over. "But no comeback, yeah?"

He slides it into the breast pocket of his jacket. "This Carter thing is a sideshow. You should be striking out on your own."

"Let's not argue about this now."

They sit quietly for a while. He touches her hands, and she smiles at him and in the brief coffee-shop sunlight glow, all is well between them.

"I gotta go," he says, standing up, straightening his suit. "But look, I've said it before, I know some people who would very much like to see a new competitor in game media, and you'd be a great leader."

"OK. Sure."

Alejandro fancies himself a mover and shaker in the media. She discourages these big plans of his. She knows what it takes to create an audience that's big enough to return its investment. It's a pipe-dream.

"Now," he says, smiling. "I gotta get back to the office. A lot of reviews to read in..." He checks his watch. "Jesus, fifteen minutes."

He looks at her and pauses as he stands. She stands too and they embrace. She won't tell him about the review, not here. She can't.

"I'll see you at the Convention Center, at 5?" she says.

"See you there," he replies, "at the big stage. Lots to do today." He makes a dorky little shuffle with his arms, signifying great industry and she laughs.

When he leaves the café, she writes a text on her phone.

I'm sorry babe. I really have a problem with this game. Let's talk about it later. Kx

She looks at the text, times the message for 3:59 p.m. delivery and presses send.

10

SATANIC REALM 5

4:00p.m.

REVIEW: Satanic Realm 5
Publisher: Saturnine
Developer: Saturnine Los Gatos

Kjersti Wong reviews Saturnine's latest trip to the underworld...

Satanic Realm has been a part of my life for as long as I can recall. My father introduced me to the first game-- no, not the official *Satanic Realm 1*, but an obscure piece of Commodore 64 shareware that was released in 1990-- and we played it from start to finish in one weekend. It was called *Dare You Enter the Devil's Lair*. Today, it is entirely forgotten. I can't even find it among the online emulation databases.

The graphics were miserly, but those puzzles delighted us: me, an 8-year-old girl and my loving dad, a 55-year-old man, happily solving fiendish ways to slay evil imps.

We spent a lot of time together in those days. My mother was often unwell, in and out of the hospital.

I remember a few months later the game was mentioned in the letters pages of a British magazine called Commodore User. My dad thought it was wonderful that the gaming community could connect this way, just by the free physical exchange of tapes and disks. He said that would be the future.

The shareware had been written by two brothers from Stevenage, England, Dan and Roy Edwards. They wrote some more games and, gradually they became more and more successful.

Later, they were contracted by a publisher in Britain called Nine Dreams and they began work on a new game for the Amiga. It too was a dungeon crawler with lots of puzzles, all new.

Satanic Realm was a sensation. I remember reading all the reviews in gorgeous magazines like Amiga Power, and wishing that I too could write about these wonderful games for a living.

But that was also a sad time for me. Terrible things were happening in my life, events that I could not fully understand, but which hurt me very much. *Satanic Realm* was an escape. I inhabited that game.

My mother and father had met while she was working in

Hong Kong. She was a sound engineer for a Norwegian TV company making a show about Asian food. He was a locally hired technician. They fell in love, married. They moved to Oslo. I was born.

As I mentioned before, she became unwell, and so we moved to her hometown, a small place outside Bergen. When I was nine, my mother passed away, taken by leukemia. After the funeral, I remember going home and playing on my Amiga. That's pretty much all I did in those days.

I have one particular photograph of her. It sits on my desk. A strong face, masses of blonde hair, a smile that stays with me every minute of every day.

A few days after the funeral, my dad bought me a SNES and, together, we discovered a whole new world of games.

My father raised me alone. He made his living fixing computers and teaching English. These were his passions. We were outsiders where we lived, but we were, mostly, popular enough. We spent our time with one another. We would play SNES or MegaDrive games or fool about with our beloved Amiga, making music or art or anything, really. We would play games.

A few years later, *Satanic Realm 2* arrived. Although there were some good moments in the game, it was confused, charmless, a great disappointment.

The Edwards brothers had formed a company and been bought by Nine Dreams. But they had not enjoyed corporate life. There had been arguments and they had quit. Their whereabouts now is unknown. I have tried to track them down, without success. As far as I know, they never made another game.

The press were merciless about *Satanic Realm 2*. In those days, they were much less forgiving than today. My father and I played the game, in part to understand what had gone wrong from a design point of view.

In any case, he had found a new passion. It was called the Internet. Together, we created a website that offered up reviews and news about games, in Norwegian. *Satanic Realm 2* was my first review (I gave it one star out of five, such was my disappointment).

A Norwegian game website was a new thing in the world, and, as much by being first to the table as because of any skill on my part, it became successful.

Throughout my high school years, I maintained this site. I remember receiving my first free games, and what a great feeling that was. I learned to write about games. My dad and I launched an English-language version of the site, which did pretty well too. Some guys in Oslo and in London sold the advertising and gave us a cut.

When I was 19, it was time for me to go to college. My father wanted me to attend one of the American universities, but we compromised. I decided to study English literature at Edinburgh University, Scotland, which, if you look at a map, is just across the water from Bergen.

We sold the website to a publishing company in Stockholm, and used the money to fund my education. Throughout that time I also freelanced for some game magazines, like

Edge in the UK and Next Generation in America. I learned a lot about writing reviews.

In my first year at university, *Satanic Realm III* arrived for PC. Nine Dreams had been going to the wall, and was merged with a struggling U.S. outfit called Saturn Publishing. The new company was called, of course, Saturnine Dreams. They took the basic Satanic Realm idea and gave it to some coders in Seattle.

The game was inventive, imaginative, a joy, a classic, with an incredible combative multiplayer mode, playable over the Internet. My father and I connected in this way, and it helped us both cope with how much we missed one another. If I say that we played for a thousand hours, I may well be underestimating.

I returned to Bergen often. It was clear that my father, who had always been a fit and robust man, was failing in his health. He had become old. He refused to allow me to quit my studies and tend to him.

He lived to see me complete my education satisfactorily. After he passed away, I spent a year at home. Once again, I turned to games. I played a lot of MMOs.

In late 2005 I decided to move to America, to San Francisco, to begin a new life, to escape from my grief. I sought out a job at the many game magazines and websites in that fine city. To each one, I sent resumes and work samples. I heard nothing. My visa was only for six months and my money soon began to run low.

Then, I decided to try something different. I hired a

videographer and told her about my situation. I wanted to make a video resume. She instructed me to dress in a certain way, to use humor and flirtatious behavior. I enjoyed making this film. We sent it to all the game companies. Within a week, I was hired, I moved to L.A. and have worked at Piranha Frenzy ever since as a video presenter.

Throughout this time Saturnine Dreams changed its name to simply Saturnine, and grew to become the biggest publisher of games in the U.S. and Europe. *Satanic Realm 4* became the game everyone most wanted to see. It was rumored to be in development, and then cancelled and so on.

Finally, the game was officially announced at G2G in 2013 and released in 2014. I persuaded the then-editor of Piranha Frenzy to allow me to review the game. Although it lacked the originality of *1* or *3*, it is still a fine game. I gave it 85% and, two years on, I still think that was a fair score.

Around this time, I met Saturnine's marketing boss, Alejandro Bernal. We became friends and, later, lovers, which we remain today.

So, here we are with *Satanic Realm 5*, which I have been playing for the past few days. In itself, this is problematic. Usually, game publishers give us more time to evaluate their games, especially when they are large and complex.

At first I found the game entertaining and diverting. But soon, it began to irritate me and eventually, it made me angry.

If you are a fan of *SR4*, and even *SR3*, you will find *Satanic Realm 5* comforting and familiar, and this may be a good thing. Certainly, I thought so, at first. And then, a weird feeling came over me, that I had played this game before. I searched my notes and those old reviews and my memories. It took me some time to get there, but eventually I realized something extremely concerning.

Satanic Realm 5 is essentially an updated version of *Dare You Enter the Devil's Lair?*. It is the same compendium of puzzles, maps, lairs and enemies, albeit with vastly improved graphics and AI.

This is a game that has already been made, by people who have been given no credit. I understand, of course, that a game in 2016 and an 8-bit game are as far apart as two games can be, in terms of how they look, the sophistication of their mechanics. But I am speaking of their soul. This is a remake, which would be fine, if the game had been pitched as such, if its original makers had been credited. But it is being sold as something new and fresh, which it is not.

Puzzles are like jokes. Once you have experienced them, they lose their flavor. I understand that many people playing the game will not have played all of the titles in the series, and very few people in the world will have played *Dare You Enter the Devil's Lair?*.

But the original game's obscurity does not excuse the game's publisher, which has clearly seen fit to create something cheaply and quickly that ought to have been created with care and imagination.

I do not have a copy of *Dare You Enter the Devil's Lair?* and, in the time given me to review this game, have not been able to find an emulated version. Indeed, there are very few mentions of the game on the Internet. But my memory of this game is faultless. When I tell you that this is a remake, I do so with absolute confidence.

Satanic Realm 5 is a pretty game, a world of color and noise that anyone can appreciate. But at its heart, it is ugly, an example of the sort of shoddy commercial practices that foul gaming today.

Game reviews are, all too often, checklists for features and their merits in comparison to competing works. The graphics, the controls, the voice-acting are all measured. In these respects, this is a decent enough game. But it is also a work of art, and a commercial offering, and in both respects it is left wanting. It would be dishonest of me to judge this game purely on its mechanistic properties, ignoring the ethical background of its formation.

If you have never played a Satanic Realm game before, then I recommend you buy the previous game in the series, which can currently be purchased for $20. If you are a person who believes in honesty and the value of originality, I am sorry to disappoint you. *Satanic Realm 5* is a fraud.

Score: 30%

11

ANGER MANAGEMENT

4:12 p.m.

"So, Kjersti. I just want to be clear about the sequence of events. You posted the review without allowing me or Brad to see a single word of the copy?"

They are seated around a table in the Small Meeting Room. Sheldon is speaking calmly, but he knows he's doing a very poor job of holding his temper.

"Can I venture to inquire why you would ignore all our established protocols to do this?" He feels his face heating up, the surging, needful panic of an impending explosion.

Kjersti looks at him directly, glances across at Brad, who is peering over his glasses like a 1980s professor-of-cool, reading the review on a printout for what Sheldon reckons to be at least the fifth time.

"You asked me to review the game," says Kjersti. "My personal opinion. A subjective appraisal. A criticism."

Sheldon tries to control himself, seeks a way to keep his voice quiet, but he knows he's losing control. He wants to yell. He feels blood pumping in his ears.

"You were told to submit copy before publication. You fucking disobeyed me." Now he is yelling.

A woman passing the office looks up at the sound of a raised voice. It's a warning sign. He knows he needs to calm down.

"Can we at least be honest, Sheldon?" says Kjersti. "It's been..." She checks her cell phone. "...thirteen minutes since the embargo dropped and the review went live. This meeting is not about established protocols. It's about the score."

Sheldon surrenders to himself, feels a happy release, a sloughing away of various internal locks and mechanisms. His mind welcomes the relief even while his reason begs him to stop. Dopamine floods his synapses.

He yells, without the slightest inhibition.

"Of course it's about the score, you fucking cunt!"

Time stops in the Small Meeting Room. A pause, a jolt, the moment in *Braid* or *TimeShift* when everything goes backward, and the world gets another go.

She cocks a cold eye at him. "Cunt?"

He gasps. There is no going backward in the Small Meeting Room, in the real world. He looks at a stricken Brad. Looks back at Kjersti. His heart is racing.

"I didn't say cunt," he says quickly. "Did I say cunt, Brad?" I said, "You... can't... You can't... do this. You fucking... can't do this to me."

"We should decide what to do about this," Brad says, quickly. He waves the piece of paper. Brad is actually shaking, not just his hands, all of him. The man is trembling with fear.

Sheldon stares at Kjersti, says a silent one-syllable prayer to the HR gods that she is not going to make trouble about what he's just said. She's old-school he thinks. European. They're more easygoing about these things. She won't run to HR and make a fuss. It'll be fine.

But he knows he can't fire her. Not right now, anyway. He rubs the bridge of his nose. Tries to remember a way to calm down. Breathing exercises?

"Please, read the review back for me, Brad," he says. "Just the last few paragraphs. Not the rest of it."

Brad begins to read, his voice quavering.

Kjersti and Sheldon stare at one another. He can see she is incensed, but that she knows how to control herself. Sheldon turns his head slowly, ashamed of his own rage, looks to Brad, who finishes off, sadly. "Score: 30%." He places the paper in front of him, fussily and neatly, face down.

The time of the reading has allowed Sheldon to gather himself, to collect his fear and to cool his incandescence. He does not want to think about the ramifications. He does not want to think about the voicemails he is sure to find on his return to his office, from his ad manager, from his CEO, from Alejandro Bernal. Jesus. He might even have to face HR. He tries to forget the ugly name he just called his pretty, semi-famous video presenter.

Sheldon decides it's better to stay on the offensive, at least to some degree. A pell-mell retreat might make her bold.

"So, where is this old Commodore 64 game? You have the evidence to show us? The clear comparative data."

"There's no evidence," she says. "I didn't have time to find a copy of the game. There's nothing online. It's too obscure. It's lost. But I remember, very clearly..."

"Memories are fallible, especially childhood memories," he says, very quietly. "It's not good enough. So, this is what happens next. Brad, pull the review. Immediately. Publish a sensible note saying that the review we posted did not meet the editorial standards expected at Piranha Frenzy, mention our ethical approach to personal relationships. Write a new review and get it up there, asap, with a score that reflects the game's actual merits, rather than Kjersti's special life memories."

Brad sits still.

Sheldon shouts, "What are you waiting for, Brad?"

"I haven't played the game, Sheldon. How can I write a review?"

Sheldon glares at him. "How long have you been doing this, Brad? We've all had to knock out a review for a game we've never played. It's not difficult. There are thirty reviews out there, averaging 80%. Read a few of them and go and write one that's just like those others. Now."

There is an unpleasant scraping sound as Brad gets up, quickly, and heads for the office door.

Kjersti is sitting very still. Sheldon knows she has to be enraged and can't help admiring the fact that, apart from her grave facial expression, she isn't trembling, shaking or showing some other manifestation of extreme anger.

"I know you're not going to be happy with this, Kjersti," he says. "But you're in the wrong here."

She's glaring at him.

"I also know you'll be smart."

"I'm right. This game is a rip-off."

"You've built a good career here, a good life."

"The review was honest."

He sighs. The time for subtlety is over, he decides. "We both know that if you quit you'll have thirty days to leave the United States and return to the longships and the fjords or whatever you people have in Norway these days."

She is still glaring at him, barely blinking. For once, he actually wants to be in a meeting where he is responsible for a woman crying. Anything would be better than this.

"You have killed a serious review because you don't trust me," she says. "And, by the way, there's a whole lot of financial gain. You'd rather suck up to the publishers."

"We killed the review because it contains an unsubstantiated libel," he says, the pitch in his voice rising. "You made an allegation of plagiarism based on a twenty-five-year-old memory and, frankly, a bunch of confused personal feelings. You look like a spoiled girl who had a fight with her boyfriend and wanted revenge or went looking for notoriety and got burned."

"I will find the evidence. Then, there will be consequences."

"Let me worry about consequences."

She does not reply.

"So here is what I think you should do," he says. "You should keep your mouth shut and do your time and trust me to look after you. You can learn from this. Let's look at this episode as a learning step. I'll look after you."

Kjersti snorts at him, turns her head in disgust.

He remembers how keen they all were to hire her, back in '06, when she'd sent in that sexy video. Just at a time when they were taking heat for never having employed a female—outside of HR and sales, anyway—and she'd turned up. This pretty Asian woman with a quaint Age of Empires accent who knew about games. Just when video was taking off. Just when their YouTube channel was growing. She was perfect.

He speaks to her now in soothing tones, "I want you to understand that Piranha Frenzy is going to be the making of you. But you cannot afford to start going off the reservation right now, especially with this particular game. You understand how this works, the real world I mean, where people like Zoe and Charlie and Liam all have to be paid every month, all have to have their insurance stumped up, month after month."

"I understand perfectly," she says, and stands.

"Don't fuck up your career," says Sheldon, looking up at her. "There are no easy passes in this business. You know that. You've come too far."

"I have not forgotten what you called me."

Sheldon considers another denial, but decides against it.

She goes through the door, and closes it very, very quietly. This alarms him more than he can say.

12

CIGARETTES

4:33 p.m.

She walks down the fire escape steps in a daze of fury, considers throwing herself against the cold hard walls. Their sick-colored paint is nauseating. She wants to scream and weep. There is nowhere for her anger to go.

She feels the tears prickling, recognizes that what she is feeling is hatred and shame, and that it must come out. She waits in a stairwell, tries to collect herself.

When the crying passes, she checks her phone. There has been nothing from Alejandro. He must have read the review. He must have seen that it had been pulled. He must know that she is in a world of shit. But she has received no messages.

She checks her email. It is full of hate messages from Satanic Realm fans, Google alerts of her name, a short-lived internal email thread from the editorial floor, debating the rights and wrongs of her review, capped by a warning from Brad to knock it off and get back to work.

Twitter will be all over this, she thinks. There won't be a blogger or an editor or even a PR person lacking an opinion.

Some will be supportive; some might even validate her memory of *Dare You Enter the Devil's Lair?* The thought occurs to her that someone, somewhere might have a copy of the game, that one of the Edwards twins will come forward. But she knows she's in trouble. that, even with all her certainty, she needs to get some evidence.

She knows too that many observers, especially those who have toed the line, who have scored the game highly, will have too much to lose by accepting her story. They will say that she got it wrong.

Her only hope is a twenty-five-year-old game. The most pursued game in the world for the next few days will be *Dare You Enter the Devil's Lair?* There is every chance that the game no longer exists. I am swinging in the wind, she thinks. I have done this to myself.

Kjersti collects herself. I have to carry on she thinks. She is due at the Convention Center where she can finally confront Alex and put her accusation to him directly, as she ought to have done in the coffee shop.

Emerging through a fire door, outside on the street, Kjersti finds Frank and Zoe sitting on a concrete ledge, smoking cigarettes. She sits beside them, puts her head in her hands. There are tears on her fingers and on her face.

Zoe rubs her back. Frank offers her a smoke, which she takes. She hasn't smoked in years. She can't look at him, at his deep lines of concern. It will make everything so much worse.

"Brad sent out an email just now," says Frank. "Saying that it's all going to be fine and we should keep our heads down. Just like the wriggling little worm that he is."

She laughs, dries her face with the heel of her hand.

"We should all just quit," says Zoe. "Right now."

"No," says Kjersti. The crying is really done now. She puffs on her cigarette, feels a welcoming swoosh of nicotine. "It was foolish of me to post that review. I had to know they would pull it and I'd wind up looking like a fool."

"You did what was right," says Frank. "We trust you. They are in the wrong. You'll see."

"I should have gotten some proof."

"Well, yes," says Frank. "But let's see what comes out in the next day or so. The Internet is a wonderful thing, or so they tell me."

"I still say we should all quit," says Zoe. "That guy at GameSpot did it. Remember that?"

"GameSpot fired him," says Frank. "They fired him for taking a stand. The others quit in support of him."

"They won't fire me," says Kjersti. She doesn't want to repeat the details of the meeting, even though she knows they are both itching to hear every word of it.

She recalls the GameSpot episode. A respected and established editor had posted a negative review of some now-forgotten action game. He had been fired by weak bosses under pressure from an advertiser.

That had been almost a decade before. The editor had been able to start up a well-funded, much admired game website called Giant Bomb. But there hadn't been many more of those opportunities in the intervening years, and there wouldn't likely be many more to come.

If she quits, she knows she cannot hope to garner the necessary sympathy and goodwill to trigger a walk-out. She will not be followed out the door by loyal team-mates keen to do the right thing. A full-time job in game journalism is a thing of value, she thinks.

Despite Zoe's bravado, Kjersti knows the young woman would rather slice off her right arm than sacrifice a plum job in game journalism. And as for Frank, at his age, he couldn't hope to land another position. It was too much to expect of anyone, especially someone as fragile as him, looking after a sick partner and one bad day away from falling back into a booze-fueled haze.

"The bastards have got us by the short and curlies," says Frank. "We can shout our mouths off all we like, but the truth is, there's not much glory in unemployment."

"Or going to work for the game companies as a shill," says Zoe, glumly.

They sit quietly for a while, smoking. "What did Brad say in his email?" Kjersti asks.

"He said the review was being pulled and replaced," says Zoe. "He said he didn't want to hear a word about it. It was definitely not awesomely awesome."

They watch people come and go through the glass doors of the office high-rise, unfamiliar faces from the legal firms, tech start-ups and movie biz offshoots that take up most of the building's floors. She checks her phone again. Nothing from Alejandro.

Charlie emerges through the doors, carrying a large cardboard box, his enormous backpack slung over his shoulder. He is grinning widely.

He ambles up to them. Kjersti can't recall seeing him outdoors in full daylight ever before, can't recall seeing him smile much. This is the first time she has seen his teeth. She thinks they could do with a good scrub.

"What's in the box, Charlie?" Frank asks. "Dead animals?"

"Kjersti," Charlie says, ignoring the remark. "Kjersti, Kjersti." He is shaking his head, slowly, a display of admiration. "That was AMAZING." He starts giggling.

"Are you talking about the review, Charlie?" Once again, Kjersti finds the boy irritating and perplexing.

"It's been pulled, fuckwit," says Zoe. "Your buddy Brad is shitting out a replacement right now."

Charlie smirks. "Oh," he says. "I know all about that. Kjersti, the way you had Sheldon screaming mad in that meeting. I can't believe he called you a cunt. He definitely said 'cunt.'"

"You heard that? You were listening?"

"What the hell is going on, Charlie?" asks Frank.

"He called you what?" says Zoe, signs of genuine outrage blooming in her face.

"I've gotta go," says Charlie. They are all on their feet now. "Can't stay here. Big bad Sheldon is going to figure out who has been doing the leaks. See you at the party, maybe."

"Hold on," says Kjersti. "You're the leak?"

He turns to her, shifting the large box under his arm. "Will you tell Sheldon?" he asks.

"No," she says.

Frank shakes his head. "Why would we?"

Zoe is still gaping at Kjersti, her face flushed with anger.

"Because I'm asking you to," says Charlie. "I want you to. First chance you get."
He waves and walks away.

"He bugged the rooms?" says Frank. "And now he's going to publish the lot online. Charlie Black is the Scourge of Corruption. That's unreal."

"Oh hell," says Kjersti. "Is he going to leak my private meeting?"

"Did you say anything regrettable?" asks Frank.

"It sounds like Sheldon did," says Zoe. "He really said that?"

"No. I don't think I said anything, I didn't say much at all," says Kjersti. "But it's what I didn't say that might screw me. The Scourge. He could make me look like an accomplice."

"You're being paranoid," says Frank. "You wrote the 30% review that they pulled. It's already all over r/games and NeoGAF. You're fine. It's Sheldon who needs to worry."

"And Brad," says Zoe. "Sheldon's little poodle."

Kjersti checks her phone again. Still nothing from Alejandro.

"I guess you've got a tough few days in front of you," says Frank. She catches something in his manner, something being held back. "I wish I could help. I'll do some digging, see if I can find out more on this old game of yours. Maybe I'll have some time now."

"You OK, Frank?"

"Yeah," he says. "Just peachy. Hey, Zoe, gimme another cigarette."

"Something's going on here," says Kjersti. "Seriously, Frank. What's wrong?"

Frank lights the cigarette. "Sheldon wants to see me. We were supposed to meet an hour and a half ago, but I guess he's been busy bullying reviewers."

"Oh no," says Kjersti. She understands immediately. "They can't let you go."

"That's crazy," says Zoe. "We need you."

"I know, Zoe. You really do. The way you misuse adjectives is a crime. But you'll manage. And Kjersti. Don't do anything rash. You can't go quitting just because Sheldon is cutting costs again. Don't get mixed up in this. You're too important to me. I'd never forgive myself."

"This is insane," Kjersti says. "It can't be true. You're too important to us."

"I hardly touch the copy these days," he says. "Too much blowback from the writers. They sulk and complain if I add even a comma. Easier just to wave it through. It's not like Piranha Frenzy's readers are complaining about editorial standards. They come for the scores and the videos and the screenshots."

"You don't believe that, Frank..."

He gazes at her. "You and I joined for the same reason, Kjersti. We wanted to work for the best game news outlet in the world. Tell me, did we succeed? Do we work for an admirable news outlet?"

She looks down. "It's... wank."

They both smile at the word.

"That should be our new slogan," says Zoe. "Piranha Frenzy... It's wank."

Frank's cell phone buzzes. He throws his cigarette away, reaches into his pocket.

"Ah," he says, looking at the screen. "Sheldon says he will be ready for me at 17:00 hours. The hour is near."

"He's not going to fire you," says Kjersti. "It's something else. Call me when it's done." But she doesn't feel any confidence in her words.

"I will," he says. "Take it easy. Be cool."

Kjersti checks her phone again. As well as a few messages from co-workers and PR friends, asking if she is OK, emails and Twitter messages are streaming in, calling her a liar and a fantasist and much, much worse.

Still nothing from Alejandro.

13

LACC

4:48 p.m.

As she makes her way through the downtown hum, toward the Los Angeles Convention Center, she passes groups of video game fans gathered in large numbers. She is recognized. A few fans wave at her, here and there, stop to say hello or call out Piranha Frenzy slogans.

"FRENZY!"

They smile and wave. It is always this way at big video game events.

Groups of game fans are milling around, wearing cosplay, some carrying banners or wearing T-shirts denoting their particular video game allegiance.

She sees some wearing *Satanic Realm 5* costumes, ranging from the intricately decorous to simple devilish headgear and tails. They are yelling and singing songs to some *Diabolic Underworld* fans, rivals, also in cosplay, also yelling in return. A few are taunting one another aggressively. The atmosphere teeters between good-natured banter and outright hostility. Security guards look on, bemused, nervous.

In recent years, the traditionally vicious online debates between fans of different games and gaming systems have somehow spilled out into the real world. G2G, once a place where gaming came together as a fraternity, to admire one another's passion and commitment, today seems more like a place where rival clans strut and crow.

She walks by a small group of women, in their late teens and early 20s, wearing *Satanic Realm 5* tees and red-horned hats. "There's Kjersti Wong," one woman shouts, dragging her friend toward Kjersti. They stand in the street, blocking her way momentarily.

"30 percent? You ignorant bitch," says the first woman, almost spitting the words. She is red-faced with anger. Kjersti stops for a moment, stares at the two women. "Liar," the other says, smirking.

Collecting herself, seeing the doors to the Convention Center a few dozen yards ahead, Kjersti pushes by.

"Kjersti Wong is wrong," the first woman chants, and soon there is a group of them, behind her, chanting, "Kjersti Wrong. Kjersti Wrong. Kjersti Wrong." They follow her all the way to the Convention Center entrance.

She has heard all this before, many times. On the forums, they accuse her of incompetence, attention-seeking, stupidity and worse. Now the vitriol has slipped the digital world and loosed itself into reality.

Kjersti enters LACC and shows her ID to a security guard. She is shaking. She remembers a conversation once with Frank, about Internet comments. "They wouldn't dare say those things to your face," he'd said. He was wrong.

She seeks out a bathroom. After sitting on a lavatory for far too long, she approaches a mirror and tries fixing herself up. She looks tired and disheveled. Dark rims under her eyes highlight her fatigue. She enters the exhibition area, keeps her head down.

Pre-G2G, LACC is a chaotic, noisy building site. Booths and stages are being erected, a strange juxtaposition of construction noises alongside gatherings of fantasy characters in every shape and size; pixies, orcs, superheroes, blobs and elongations smiling, snarling and snooping.

Among the buzzing tools and saws, Kjersti picks her way across a broken terrain of rolled-up indigo carpets, pallets loaded with lighting and audio equipment.

Wrapped statues of gigantic video game characters, stilled in their moments of rage and violence, are laid face-down in the aisles.

A sense of determined urgency is evident on the faces of the construction workers. Within less than twenty-four hours, the public will be thronging through here.

As she walks about the Convention Center, she sees what each game's publisher and hardware manufacturer has planned for the show. There are mammoth-sized posters everywhere.

She crosses a massive open-arena surrounded on three sides by a vast, quasi-fascistic stage, festooned with giant screens. The screens and mics are being tested by engineers. Dancers are on the stage, practicing their moves.

This stage is supposed to be her home for the next few days. As G2G's primary official media outlet, she hosts the onstage reveals for Piranha Frenzy, handles interviews and audience activities, with help from Steve and now Liam.

It is probable, she thinks, that even now Sheldon and Brad are talking about keeping her out of the public eye for the duration of the show.

Alejandro is on the stage, speaking to a choreographer and the surrounding group of dancers. They are showing off a new dancing game. Such displays are a staple of game shows.

There is laughter. His team is happy, and he is busy, she thinks—too busy to reply to her text.

As he sees her approaching, he takes his leave of the dancers, climbs down from the stage. Since their earlier meeting, he has taken off his suit jacket and tie, his sleeves are rolled up.

For a moment, she is reminded of Hollywood musicals, the man-of-action pulling together a grand show. "Are you OK?" he asks, touching her waist, but not kissing her.

"No. No, I'm not OK." She looks at him levelly. "I'm having a lousy day. I suppose you saw my review?"

"I did," he says. "Interesting theory."

"Did you tell Sheldon to pull the review?"

His face registers genuine surprise. "Of course not. My PR people are going nuts about it."

"Surely this is what you people want? A bad review torn down and replaced with a good one."

"You people?" He flashes a look of annoyance at her. "You need to calm down, Kjersti. None of this is my fault. I'm the one who ought to be mad here."

"So you are angry about my review."

"No. Well, yes. That crazy stuff about us copying some old game, it's all people are talking about. Your review is everywhere."

He begins walking, back toward the stage, and she follows. The floor is crammed with people messing around with cables and carpeting.

"More people will read my review than any other." She says this dully, without any joy or pride. Her review is already tainted. It is no longer about her or about her father or about the game. It is about something else, something ugly.

"I know you think I'm angry that you gave it a shitty score, but I'm not. I'm angry that you reviewed the game at all."

"You don't care about the score? Come on," she says, skeptically. "You live for the scores, for Metacritic. Every percentage point is worth dollars."

"That's not what I'm talking about," he says, turning to her. They stand next to a giant sack filled with thousands of hand-sized fluffy toys, wrapped in cellophane, all bright colors: coins, toads, bears, turtles, bricks, stars, hammers.

"Your review is just one of dozens. You giving it that horrible score takes the average down by a notch or two. It's not the end of the world. But now, because of Sheldon's incompetence, it's become the only review that matters. That moron. He's left me about twenty messages already. Who uses voicemail?" He trails off and is looking up at the stage, frowns at some imperfection in the set-up.

"I had to write the review I believed in," she says.

"I told you that it was a mistake for you to take this on. There are too many agendas playing out here. Stuff you don't understand. That's been your mistake. That's all."

"I'm a fucking game reviewer," she says, loudly. "I was the right person to take on that review, the only person. Everything else is irrelevant." She's shouting. Some workers look up.

Alejandro looks hard at her, glances around, leans forward. "Do you want someone to video us together, arguing like this?"

She shakes him off and walks away from the giant sack of fluffy toys.

Of course there'd been conversations at the office, about her relationship, about the review. Frank had argued that it might be seen as a conflict. Others had said it shouldn't make a difference. Some, she thought now with discomfort, had stayed silent, had waited for it all to play out.

She'd won the argument by pointing out that if her relationship with Alex biased her toward his games, it would follow that she would be biased against all competing games, in which case, the logical conclusion would be that she should cease reviewing games, or writing about them at all.

But she knows that she'd been given the review because Brad and Sheldon assumed she'd be soft on any of its flaws.

Alejandro catches her up, steers her toward the stage. "Let's find somewhere private," he says. The music and shouting is deafening.

Since the beginning of game magazines, there had been reviewers (almost always male) who had unhealthily close relationships with people working in PR, usually unacknowledged. It had been going on for years, and yet, a blind eye was turned. But her open relationship with Alejandro had been deemed a problem. This hypocrisy, she knows, pushed her harder toward insisting on taking the review.

They climb onto the stage and shuffle past the dancers. Alejandro leads her backstage into a corridor, past a security guard. Engineers cluster in dark rooms, setting up the video and audio equipment for tomorrow's opening ceremony. Finally they step into a very small office.

"I spoke to our PRs just before you got here," he says, closing the door and offering her the sofa. "We've already made the request to Piranha Frenzy that you re-review the game, with our added assurance that the core allegation you made is just not true, and that one part of it is taken out."

"That's the only part that matters," she snorts. "You're denying that the game is a rip-off?"

"It's crazy, Kjersti. It's senseless. Where is this corny old game?"

"I remember it," she says. "The puzzles, the plot, the humor—it's all the same."

"Kjersti, you've made a very serious accusation. You need to have proof. They didn't teach you that at journalism school?"

She glares at him.

"But, me and you," he says, "it complicates things. It makes Saturnine's request to reinstate the review less about fairness and a noble acceptance of diversity of opinion, and more about that fact that we're..."

"I get it," she says. They sit silently for a few moments. He hands her a bottle of water.

"You're finished at Piranha Frenzy. That's certain," he says. "They'll find a way to get you out—maybe not today, but soon. You have to do what I have been saying for months," he says, stroking her arm. "You have to quit and start afresh. If you stay, you'll always be seen as a lapdog. But if you go, you can be a lion. Lick your wounds. Move on."

"Ever the marketing-friendly allusion," she says, smiling weakly. She feels nauseous. She thinks again of her dad's boxes of cassettes, how much she needs him now, to tell her that she's not crazy.

"You know I'm right," says Alejandro.

She says nothing.

"Quit today," he says.

"And admit that I'm wrong? Then what? Hello unemployment. Hello no-visa. Hello Norway."

"I told you before, there are people who would love to get something launched against trash like Piranha Frenzy. They want to see something new, they want to be a part of that scene, and they want to have a piece of the media. I know people. I can get some backers."

"Why, Alex? Why would they trust me? I just unloaded on the biggest game of the summer and, according to you, based the whole thing on a childish memory."

He waves it away. "It's an error. The game will sell. A few people who might have bought it won't. But it'll still sell by the millions. You can't seriously think a multi-million dollar project can be derailed by one review? Some of you reviewers honestly think that what you create is somehow equivalent to what we create."

"You create advertising," she says.

"Not the ads. I mean, the games we make. They are incredibly expensive, complicated, they have enormous power. What is a review? It is the work of parasites..."

He sees her look of outrage... "Let me finish, Kjersti. Reviewers are just proxies for consumers, for the gamers who are too lazy to make up their own minds. They outsource the decision-making to a few reviewers. It's not art. It's process. It's a factory system for sorting out what the consumer culture will or won't accept."

He is always angry about the media. She wonders why this relationship is still going, why she is still spending her time with a man who scorns her profession.

"If the work I do is so trivial, why all the effort?" she asks. "Why all the PR, the schmoozing, the cajoling, the bullying?"

"Because it all adds up," he says, his palms stretched out, as if he were offering her an invisible box. "Because we all have to do our jobs, have to take as much control as we can find. But individually? Even a review like yours, even something that blows up, it's nothing compared to all the billboards and the TV spots and the retail posters and the Facebook campaigns. You in the media make me laugh. You think you're the big dog. You're not. You're insects. We have to keep you in mind, but you're still fleas. PR is basically pest control."

She thinks about all the calls and emails she's ever received from PR people, wheedling, complaining, pitching, suggesting—any trick they can find to edge up the score. Is it really like some vast anthill, tiny shifts in attitude and opinion moved uphill like millions of minuscule nuggets of shit?

"If you hold the media in such contempt," she asks, "why are you so keen to get your friends together to launch something else?"

"Piranha Frenzy is a crummy operation run by crummy people. But there are two things about it that my friends really like. One, it's a portal to consumers and two, it makes money."

"I wouldn't be so sure about that," she says.

He laughs. "Even your numbskull bosses can make a buck out of twenty million sets of eyeballs a month. Now, let's make some plans for you. We have to move quickly and decisively."

This too, she thinks, his love of schemes and plots. It's not about her. It's about his ego. He wants to be in control of this crisis. What better way than to possess the person at the center of the controversy?

She wants to go home, and sleep. But Alex is talking to her, urgently, making arguments. He's actually pitching to her, her own future. She hasn't the energy to argue. She nods, drinks her water and looks at the floor.

14

THE PURPLE FOLDER

5:02 p.m.

Sheldon sits quietly in the Big Meeting Room. He is not in his usual chair, which rests empty by the door. He eyes it with a certain nostalgia, and shifts uncomfortably in one of the smaller, standard-issue chairs. He is exactly midway along the table.

The only other person in the room is Pamela from HR. They are side by side, staring straight ahead at a row of empty chairs.

A folder is on the desk an inch in front of her neatly folded hands, her expertly manicured fingernails. The two of them say nothing. They have done this many times before. It is better not to be chitchatting when the third person, the victim, enters this room.

Sheldon is imagining a distressing near-future scenario in which he is in this very same room, but is sitting opposite Pamela, in the victim's chair. He imagines her flipping through her notes and asking him, in her most formal way, to confirm that he called a female employee a "cunt."

Self-loathing sweeps through his being. The idea of this lady, this perfectly tidy paragon of self-control and professionalism, looking at him while she says it, while her mouth forms the distasteful word.

His mind plays with the scenario. His claim that he was misheard would be disregarded. His argument that he has been calling male game reviewers "fucking pricks" for at least a decade with nary a hint of HR involvement would be brushed aside with a sad shake of her lovely HR head.

Sheldon's understanding of employment law is advanced enough to understand that Pamela "would have no choice," but to submit a "recommendation for action of termination" or whatever grim verbiage is favored in such circles these days.

Meanwhile, back in the current nightmare timeline, the one that is actually destroying his life, word has come back, via a staffer chatting with a PR rep, that Saturnine's natural anger about Kjersti Wong's review has been eclipsed by a far greater apoplexy generated by Sheldon's decision to replace it with some anodyne words from Brad Hoffman and a limp 85% score.

In his wrathful desire to do something to rectify the original mishap, he has failed to fully appreciate the reaction of the mob, to anticipate the frenzy currently taking place on Reddit. NeoGAF, Twitter, YouTube and even—the shame paralyzes him— via gleefully assembled editorials currently oozing from Piranha Frenzy's rivals.

In his mind he ticks off the names of the outraged journalists who will inevitably add their two cents to the unfolding scandal. Each of them fills him with loathing. The words are out before he can stop them.

"Those fucking douchebags."

Slowly, Pamela turns her head to look at him. He looks at her. She turns back to regard the empty chairs in front of them. Further humiliation is avoided by the door opening.

Frank steps in, takes in the two of them, the folder on the desk, and does a stage-clown "ta-da."

He takes his seat, the dark joke fading in the room.

"What was it, Sheldon?" says Frank. "Just got tired of my sad, old face?"

"It's nothing personal," says Sheldon.

"Right. And I'm a pink giraffe."

Pamela begins speaking. "This has been a very hard decision, but we..."

"Look love," says Frank, "I know you've got a job to do, but why don't you just leave the paperwork here and let me see if I can't figure it out for myself. See if I can decipher what all the squiggly lines mean..."

She looks at Sheldon and he nods, so she gets up, walks toward the door.

"Jesus, Pamela," says Frank. "Look, I'm so sorry. That was unnecessary. You don't deserve that."

She stops and smiles, not unkindly. "It's fine, Frank. I know how tough this is. It's tough. You can call me anytime to discuss the exit package." She leaves the room, closes the door behind her, as if she were leaving a hospital room containing a sleeping child.

"I'll call her, to apologize properly," says Frank. "That was rotten of me."

It occurs to Sheldon that he needs to speak to Kjersti. That he needs to apologize. An apology might just make things better.

Sheldon gets back to the matter at hand, forms a look on his face that says he understands how stressful these situations are. He is not as good at this as Pamela. Those people really earn their dough, he thinks.

Frank smiles back. "You know what, Sheldon? Right now I could leap over this table, fuck you up, and then happily expire of a coronary."

Sheldon chuckles. "I don't doubt it, Frank." He is relieved to be able to drop the faux sympathy. "Heck, it might even do me good to have my ass kicked. Of course, I got a lot of that in school, being the local fat fuck, so, y'know nothing new, particularly."

"Yeah," says Frank. "I see the bullied schoolboy in you. You'll get them back in the end, eh, Sheldon? One fired editor at a time."

"You're being ridiculous, Frank. I have a budget. We're just about the last game website to indulge the luxury of a copy editor. You must have known this wouldn't last forever."

Frank studies his own hands. Sheldon looks too. They are the hands of an old man.

"Your writers are mostly shit; you know that, right? They're barely literate. Even the EIC writes like a 12-year-old. There's a reason why you need a copy editor. You hired too many cheap writers. You're going to get found out."

Sheldon sighs, fiddles with the corner of the purple folder.

"Who do you think we're writing for, Frank?" he says "Do you believe these readers who come to Piranha Frenzy give a fuck how parentheses work? Do they care if 'Sega' is in uppercase or not? They are here to look at the screenshots and watch the videos and insult each other in comments. They don't give a damn, so why should I spend 70 Gs a year on you?"

Frank looks upward to the ceiling. "I think if I'd been a lickspittle, like good old Brad, I might not be losing my job today."

"Maybe. But you'd have been fired eventually. Jesus, Frank. We write about video games. You're an old man."

"As you will be, soon enough."

Sheldon's phone buzzes. He looks at it, hoping to see Alejandro's name. It's Steve, calling again, following up on some new hell Sheldon has been trying to ignore about an argument in the studio and a YouTube video. He sends the call to voicemail.

"I feel pretty old right now," he says to Frank. "These people wear you down. I'm not planning on sticking around. I've been through four sales of this company—four—picked up a few bucks along the way. One more, a big one, and I'm out."

Frank slow claps, smirks at the publisher. "You'd better hope nothing goes horribly wrong. You better hope someone doesn't knife you in the back."

"Is it you, Frank? Have you been talking to Don Roby?"

Frank laughs. "Come on, Sheldon. If I wanted to hurt you guys, I wouldn't go through a nut like Roby."

Sheldon shrugs. "I'd love to know who it is."

"It's Charlie Black," says Frank.

Sheldon is genuinely surprised. The information excites him, the sense that, knowing who the villain is, Sheldon can take control.

"Yeah? Really? Charlie? Why?"

"Can't think what his motivation might be. I mean, you treat your people so well

Sheldon. Where can this display of disloyalty be coming from?"

Sheldon ignores this sarcasm. He's already moved on to the action he needs to take, trying to figure out why Charlie is working with Don Roby. Maybe Charlie has just resurrected the bitter old fool's blogging alter ego, like some deranged copycat killer. "Charlie's a fantasist. Discrediting him will be easy. All those goofy stories he's been running..."

"Which you waved through..."

"Me? No, Frank. I leave that sort of thing to the managing editor, who is, alas, no longer with us."

They sit quietly for a few minutes.

Frank looks about the room. "I began my career in 1978, on a small newspaper in Adelaide. Did you know that? I reckon the whole operation was in a room half the size of this one."

Sheldon worries that the conversation is going to turn out to be longer than he expected. Now, all he wants to do is kill this Charlie thing and try, once again, to get Alejandro Bernal on the line. The termination of Frank Arnold has been less pleasurable than he'd hoped.

"My first editor," says Frank. "My boss back then, every now and again he would get some angry advertiser on the phone, bitching about a story they didn't like or a story they did like but that didn't go high enough or whatever. My editor had a very eloquent way with such people."

"Go on, Frank," Sheldon sighs. "Tell me. What did the great old mentor say, back in Adelaide?"

"He told them to take their advertising money and shove it up their fucking arses."

They both chuckle. "I should try that," says Sheldon. "I really should. But tell me, Frank, how's that newspaper doing today?"

Frank stands up, walks away. "Goodbye, Sheldon."

"Your folder," says Sheldon. He picks it up, but some of the loose papers slip out of his fingers, some of the pages lay splashed across the table, the legalese, the medical insurance, the weak words of thanks. He stands and scrambles to pull them together.

"It's 2016," says Frank. "Your glorious digital epoch. Just email it to me."

15

GIGANTIC DEVIL

5:45 p.m.

Kjersti turns a corner dominated by a giant Pac-Man. She spots Liam a few dozen yards ahead standing beneath an indoor crane that's midway through positioning a giant statue of Satan. She stops and watches from a distance. The camera guys are getting B-roll footage of the G2G setup for a teaser Liam's presenting.

She checks her phone for any messages from Frank. Nothing. He's promised to let her know if anything major went down at the meeting. This silence must be good, she thinks, right? The meeting, surely, was just some nonsense about G2G.

She joins the team. Liam is goofing an off-the-cuff stills montage of himself with Satan. Angie and the camera guys are all laughing.

He's going to be a joy to work with, she thinks, unlike Steve, forever complicating things, standoffish, needy for compliments, grudging with praise for others.

The crew gets serious when they see Kjersti. She tries to smile, to look normal. She's already checked her face in the bathroom, but somehow, she still feels tear-streaked and morose. She doesn't want to be doing camera work.

"If I'm crushed to death by a giant video game character, d'ya think they'll erect a statue of me?" Liam says to camera. He affects a pose like the devil, looming down over the camera, all mock-evil. The camera is on.

Angie asks Kjersti if she wants to do the same, but she demurs. "I've had enough *Satanic Realm 5* for one day," she says, and they laugh politely.

The camera off, the technicians in a huddle, Liam takes her aside. "I know I'm the new guy here," says Liam. "But every person I've talked to, including these guys here, are on your side." Members of the crew are packing away their gear, ready to move on to the next job on their checklist.

"Thanks," says Kjersti, slotting herself into professional mode as best she can. "I guess all we can do is just get on with the job at hand."

In the days ahead, most of the show will take place at various locations around G2G, including the main stage. Liam has agreed to share the work. He seems comfortable for a guy who has never performed in front of a live audience before.

"Aren't we supposed to be rehearsing in front of the Activision stage right now?" she asks. "Where's Steve? It's his slot, the new Call of Duty, right?"

"Ah. Steve," says Angie, giving Kjersti a meaningful look.

"Yeah, I guess you're not the only drama today," says Liam.

"Explain please?" says Kjersti.

Liam digs a tablet out of a backpack and taps the YouTube app. She recognizes the footage immediately, a slightly edited version of the file she'd given to Alex a few hours before.

She looks at the view count. It's already at over 12,000. The first comment reads, "I always knew this guy was a dick." The second reads, "hes the only 1 with the fukin guts to speek the truth."

"This is bad," she says. She doesn't know what else to say.

"We've got a leak in the office," says Angie, shrugging. "That's life. He's only got himself to blame."

"Where is he now?"

"Whining to Sheldon, probably," says Angie. "But I sent him a text telling him to be here on time, or we'd drop him from the show. So my guess is, he'll be here."

Kjersti doesn't want to face Steve. She doesn't know if she even wants to work at Piranha Frenzy any more. Alejandro had told her that she has no choice but to quit.

"You don't have an option," he'd argued.

She doesn't fully believe Alejandro's golden predictions of new opportunities. He doesn't understand that Piranha Frenzy is her home.

"They are plotting your assassination right now." Alejandro had said. "You have to do it first. You must pick the right time, and you have to stick the knife in, hard." He had suggested a plan, and she had nodded, not really able to offer a better alternative, but not wanting to commit to anything rash. She'd actually said to Alejandro that "the situation is fluid," for which he had given her a look of withering pity.

The video team huddles together to talk about some of the interviews lined up tomorrow. Liam asks if she is OK. She says, "Yeah, I'm fine."

Steve rounds a corner, picking his way past the Sega booth. His demeanor, even from a distance, is grim.

The guys working on the Satan statue are yelling instructions at one another. A truck noisily moves the statue into place on a plinth. They all move a few yards, to give the workers some room.

"You're late, Steve," says Angie, stating a fact, rather than judgment. "Look, we've got some tech shit to deal with here, then we're hauling over to Activision. Kjersti and Liam will get you up-to-date on the schedule, and where you slot in. Just be prepared. Activision have some PRs waiting there for the rehearsal."

And with that the production guys are gone, lumbering through the aisles, burdened under bags of gear and tripods, leaving the three presenters alone.

"Can I just ask you guys straight," says Steve, in an evidently rehearsed gambit. "Did either of you leak that video?"

Kjersti feels tentacles of guilt grip her stomach. I should not have done this to him, she thinks. He's angry and hurt. This is going to be an unpleasant conversation.

"Let's leave out the accusations, eh, Steve?" says Liam. "When the leaked slot was filmed, I left right afterwards. I haven't been back to the studio. And I know for a fact that Kjersti here has had a pretty busy day, one that's at least as rough as yours. So..."

Steve turns his eyes to Kjersti, waits for a response.

She can feel shame rising in her face. Any satisfaction that Steve is tasting a seriously negative public reaction is buried beneath the knowledge that she did this thing for all the wrong reasons.

"How bad is it?" she asks, her voice catching in her throat.

"I asked you a question." He is still staring at her, glaring really.

"And I have no intention of answering you," she says, meeting his eyes.

"Why not?" His face twitches.

"Things get leaked and sometimes they don't make us look as good as we would wish," she says. "The best thing you can do is ride it out."

"I think you did it," says Steve, his voice raised.

There is a long silence between them, just the background noise of the indoor crane and echoing voices of convention booth workers.

"This is not a law court, Steve," says Liam. "It's a game convention, and we have a lot of work to do. We can launch a full inquiry back at the office."

"Why did you do it?" he asks. "What do you hope to gain from this?"

Revenge? Justice? Malice? Cold calculation? All of the above, she thinks.

"You did it yourself, Steve," says Kjersti. "You wrote the monologue. You lost your temper. People are tired of ugly opinions."

"You fucking..."

Liam grabs him by the shoulder, gives him a gentle push, just enough to disrupt balance. "Calm down, Steve," says Liam. There is violence in his voice. His face is very close to Steve's.

"Don't tell me what to do," Steve seethes, shaking Liam loose. They stand and glare at each other.

"The one good thing about this is how much support I'm getting online," says Steve, dusting himself off, stepping away from Liam. "There are plenty of people who agree with me."

"About what?" asks Kjersti, incredulous.

"There's talk online of a protest, here at G2G tomorrow," says Steve. "People are coming out in support of free speech." He gives them both a triumphant look.

"Strictly speaking," says Liam, "it's a counter-protest. I believe some folks are already planning to demonstrate against intolerance and bullying. Not that I'm accusing you of being an intolerant bully, Steve, at all."

Protests? At G2G? Kjersti is alarmed. There is potential for trouble. The source of the leak will be more urgently investigated. Online hysteria she can handle. But if this stuff spills into the real world... The idea appalls her.

The statue is in its correct place at last. The truck starts beeping its reverse gear. Under the critical gaze of a worker in a cherry picker, they all move out of its way.

Kjersti is relieved to see Angie walking back to them, flipping through an iPad. If she notices the tension between them, she chooses to ignore it.

"The PRs are running late," says Angie. "I guess you're up to speed, Steve. From experience, there's usually something that goes to hell, so make sure you're always reachable."

"Sure," says Steve. "Sure." His face is crimson. Kjersti takes the opportunity to grab Liam's arm and guide him away. She feels his arm trembling.

"A fight on my first day," he says. "Wonderful."

"It's understandable that he'd be angry," she says.

"Will he be fired?"

"Doubt it," she says. "If I know our readers, at least half of them will be saying he's a comedy genius with every right to..."

"...do some good old-fashioned queer-bashing?"

"Well, yes. Comments will be raging right now. It won't be pretty."

"And management?"

"Sheldon's a pussy when it comes to this stuff. He won't fire Steve. The readers will be squawking about the evils of political correctness. He's terrified of looking like a liberal elitist."

Liam guffaws. "Sheldon Tavernier is about as liberal as Liz Cheney's pit bull."

They turn a corner into a quiet corridor behind the big booths, and head toward a concession stand, where dozens of empty tables await the coming hordes. They buy drinks and take a seat.

"I was always going to be a divisive figure here," says Liam. "Just didn't think it would go down like this. I thought it would be more...subtle."

"Subtle? This is the game industry."

"Did you think about that when you leaked the video?" asks Liam, turning to look directly at her.

She meets his gaze. "I don't know what I was thinking. I was angry and, I suppose, I was afraid. I took some bad advice."

He nods. "It'll pass, I guess."

"It's just... I..." She wants to talk, to open up. She's done listening to others. But she pauses. She needs a friend, but she hardly knows this man. She needs Frank.

"Go on," says Liam.

She feels a text message arriving, in her pocket. It's from Zoe.

Frank's been fired. Bastards.

She stares at it, re-reads the message just to make sure she hasn't misunderstood.

"I'm sorry Liam. I have to make a call." She tries to call Frank. Direct to voicemail. "Frank," she says, "Call me as soon as you can. Please."

When she puts the phone away, she stares into the distance.

"Everything OK?"

"No," she says. "They fired my best friend."

She can feel him watching her, waiting for her reaction.

"They can all go and fuck themselves," she says. "I'm quitting Piranha Frenzy."

He stands up, digs into his back pocket, pull out his wallet. "Another coffee? Or something stronger?"

16

CLAPTRAP

7:12 p.m.

Charlie Black lives a solitary life. He spends his time reading blogs, posting comments, editing fan videos, working. He socializes with his Piranha Frenzy teammates only when he believes it will yield something useful for his project. The only person he speaks to, regularly, is his father, via Google Chat.

But he has cultivated a hobby, or more accurately, a part-time job, under yet another pseudonym, Niko Yorda.

There is an agency in Hollywood called Excelsior Costume, which has been in business since the 1920s. It rents out costumes for parties, mostly movie-related, but it also provides appropriately garbed human decorations for grander gatherings.

It has long been Piranha Frenzy's habit to hire this agency for the company's annual G2G party, always held on the top floor of The Ale Yard a few hundred yards from L.A. Convention Center, always on the evening before the show's official opening. For game industry insiders, it's a must-attend event. Publishing bigwigs mingle with talented developers, agents schmooze with analysts. Media types gossip and plot.

This year, the theme of the evening is robots, and so, at an early hour of the evening, a large number of the hired individuals roaming the large empty hall are dressed as Optimus Prime, HK-47, Metal Sonic, Marvin, Bender, Mega Man, Clank and a Violin-Playing Toyota Robot.

(Strictly speaking, Mega Man is a cyborg, not a robot, an observation that is destined to be made on a number of occasions tonight. But, no matter.)

This is why Charlie Black enters the 2016 Piranha Frenzy G2G party through a trade entrance, dressed as the robot Claptrap, comedy relief star of the Borderlands games.

Charlie's place at the agency has been secured by his insights into video game culture and he has enjoyed his elevated status during the planning of this event.

Usually he roams fancy business parties dressed as a fruit, a car, a pop icon, or some dandy representative of any decade you care to pick, right back to the 1700s.

Black has spent some months perfecting the art of recording chattering Hollywood and business types at various lavish parties, sidling up at opportune moments and working whatever recording equipment he has been able to secrete within the folds and compartments of his costume.

With Claptrap—this costume was his own suggestion—he has no worries about where to hide cameras. Claptrap's face is a camera. The robot also features two slim, metallic arms, simple devices operated by Black's hands, inside the main casing of the robot. Buried in the left-hand side of these protrusions is a microphone.

Charlie / Lars Roby / Niko Yorda / Claptrap sees Sheldon arriving with the company CEO and the woman who runs the advertising department. They head to the bar and take a few moments to relax together before the guests arrive. Many of the partygoers will be advertising clients who will need to be impressed with the usual chummy fawning.

The room is filling up now, large parties from different companies arrive together, the noise of the room heads toward hubbub pitch.

Charlie decides to head to the bar, takes a circuitous route so he can approach the three of them from behind, but his luck is out. The ad manager and CEO spy someone of import and make their way eagerly across the room.

Charlie loiters awhile in robot mode and amuses some guests with arm waves, ignoring their requests to say something funny.

Then he sees Brad, unusually well dressed in a casual jacket and jeans, heading straight to Sheldon. The timing is good. The Scourge of Corruption's blog post must go up in a few minutes, thinks Charlie.

He has set the post to auto-publish. He wants to hear their reaction to the post, to make a recording. He feels a sharp tingle of excitement as he approaches them.

Once within listening range, he realizes that they're talking about the raving fool Steve Carter, about his unfortunate YouTube leak. Charlie doesn't care about Steve. It's a distraction. He wants them to be talking about the Scourge, about the blog post.

An auto-alert goes off on Charlie's cell phone. It's his "blog post successfully published" alarm. Dammit.

Frantically, he moves his arms inside the tight outfit, trying to get to his phone, which is in his shorts pocket. The fit is awkward; he twists and turns inside the outfit. The alarm is not turning itself off.

Sheldon and Brad turn to look at the source of the noise. Their faces register confusion. The alarm's theme tune is "Chrono Trigger"—entirely inappropriate for

Claptrap.

Charlie curses himself for forgetting to disable the alert. As he turns away from Brad and Sheldon, he can see that they recognize the tune, that they are curious as to why a random, hired costume goon would make use of such a cult video game tune.

Charlie makes a general, panicking move away from the two bosses. He finally gets his fingers around the phone and slides the volume button to mute.

He turns back to the two men. They have their own alerts to attend to. They are checking their phones. It's 8:00. He knows they are looking at the Scourge's website; he knows exactly what they, and probably every other employee of Piranha Frenzy is reading.

Blog Post: The Scourge of Corruption
For the past few months I have been gathering evidence, via a planted employee, of gross corruption within the walls of game website Piranha Frenzy. These include the willing publication of patently false stories, callous disregard for readers and scandalous collusion with game marketers, including a sordid sellout to a leading executive from Saturnine.

My original plan was to submit these to you in the traditional form of a blog post, but my plant has successfully gathered video and audio evidence that entirely support my allegations. The video is called "The Rotten Corruption at the Heart of Video Game Reviews." It will be published live, here and on my YouTube channel, at 11 a.m. Pacific Time, tomorrow. Enjoy.
-The Scourge of Corruption

Charlie moves toward the bar, where the two men are standing very close together. He stands between them and some young women in red G2G polo shirts, who are ordering drinks. The bartender looks at Claptrap. Charlie waves his mechanical arms to attract the women's attention, but they ignore him, so he extends the left arm toward the back of Sheldon's head, turns, and swivels the camera up a few degrees, to catch Sheldon and Brad's heads.

Sheldon sighs deeply and says, "A fucking video? Dear God."

Charlie can hear him fine. The audio is going to be good. The video, the backs of their heads, not so good, but it'll do.

Brad is still looking at his cell phone. "So Charlie's not just been spying on us, he's been actually bugging the offices, videos of us in the office, in meetings—is this what we're looking at here?"

Sheldon puts his hand to his head.

"This is really bad," he says. He takes a long drink. "The fact that Saturnine is mentioned. Really bad. Holy shit. Alejandro Bernal is coming tonight. He's going to rip my head off. Please Lord, kill me now."

"But what can he have, specifically?" Brad says. "What is this about colluding with game publishers? It's all lies."

Sheldon turns to Brad. "Seriously? Are you really that dumb, Brad? We almost got on our fucking knees and blew Bernal, and it sounds like Black and Roby have got that on tape. Now we've pulled a critical review and you have posted a non-critical one in its place."

"Now hold on..."

"Gah, I feel violated. To think of that little bastard recording our meetings. There must be a law against this. Corporate espionage."

"How the hell has he managed it?" says Brad. "I mean, did he bug the rooms, our desks, did he just hide under the table?"

The two men look at one another and then turn their heads, slowly, toward Claptrap. The camera looks back at them, just for a moment.

Charlie turns and runs. He makes panicked little steps inside the costume, making for the trade door, where the waiters are coming and going with hors d'oeuvres. If he can just make it to the door, if he can just make it to the working areas, away from the public.

"Stop that fucker." Sheldon is yelling. There's a pull on Charlie's shoulder, he feels himself going down, but he shakes his body wildly, the metal arms flailing around, and he feels a dislocation, a break and he hears a cry of pain, looks back, briefly. It's Brad, holding his face, injured by Claptrap's flying hand, inside of which is his mic. Brad's sunglasses are on the floor, broken.

Charlie runs past people holding drinks, looking on in alarm or amusement at the spectacle of a man chasing a robot.

Finally, Charlie sees the door, barges his way through, a waiter, side-stepping expertly as the little robot crashes into a working kitchen. He's seen this in the movies, just keep running through the kitchen. He tries to recall—where is the back door?

He's free. Brad has been accosted by kitchen staff. The catering people know that the robot is one of them; they block any stranger who dares to enter their domain.

Charlie finds an exit and is out on the street, walks a few blocks, briskly. No one cares if he's a robot. This is L.A. This is G2G. He approaches a hotel, climbs into a taxi.

The driver looks at him in the mirror, smiles, says, "Where to pal? Pandora?"

17

TIME TRAVEL

8:06 p.m.

Alone on a secluded VIP balcony, Sheldon takes a deep drink from a bottle of Pale Ale and gazes out at a bustling L.A. Live, the concrete and neon homeland for out-of-town conventioneers to while away the leisure hours before they can climb drunkenly into their hotel beds.

Sheldon would love nothing more than to slump into a taxi, slur his home address, and leave this day behind.

His irate CEO and the fizzingly enraged sales manager had witnessed the Charlie Black debacle and had quickly unburdened themselves of their opinions about the Claptrap chase and the impending video. Both of them seemed to be under the impression that all this could have been avoided if it wasn't for the unfortunate fact that Sheldon had been born and had remained, all his life, a completely incompetent fucktard.

Having taken his licking—he realized it just made them feel better—he resolved to figure out a way to survive the impending reputation catastrophe bearing down on his career. He decides that getting the better of his executive rivals can wait, for now.

In the interim, he wallows, he drinks, he takes solace in a precious moment of Sheldon-time, a tasty beer, a few minutes away from the appalled gaze of staff members, the polite inquiries of clients, the brazen mockery of rivals.

In truth, he realizes, the one place he really wants to be right now is not his home in Santa Monica, but his mom's front room in Petersham, Massachusetts, just after breakfast on Christmas morning, 1985, opening up his first NES, playing *Super Mario Bros.*

He is leaning against a railing, looking out. Behind him, he hears a brief burst of music and party babble as the balcony door opens and closes. He hopes it's just some wandering guest who will leave him alone. To encourage retreat, he does not turn.

Sheldon yearns to return to the happy certainties of his childhood, the tinkling simplicity of Super Mario Bros. He wants to restart, to stamp on all the bad things, soar above the pettiness, wipe over his own errors.

If that's not possible, if 1985 is unreachable, perhaps he can go back to his first college year, playing *X-Wing*, *Syndicate* and *The 7th Guest* in his dorm room. It was then, in the early-'90s glow, that he had come to the decision that he would one day work in video games, because it would be fun and fulfilling.

He thinks how he could even have saved himself, if he could go back just as far as his appointment as editor-in-chief of Piranha Frenzy, to the days of *Majora's Mask* and *Perfect Dark* and *Diablo II*. How he had seemed on the precipice of greatness then, an EIC at age 25, after just three years on the editorial floor. He had been confident in his own moral nobility, his own ability to choose the right way forward, his own...

"A moment's reflection?"

Sheldon recognizes the voice behind him, immediately. His body stiffens as he turns, realizing as he does that he's making no attempt to fix a smile on his face.

"Alejandro."

Bernal offers his hand to shake. He is wearing what Sheldon understands to be a very fine suit, and carrying a glass that could be filled with a clear vodka cocktail but is probably water. Standing with his bottle of beer, his blanket-like clothes, Sheldon feels like an oaf.

Saturnine's urbane marketing chief is offering his very best shit-eating grin, which Sheldon knows is designed to transmit the message that this is going to be an extremely unpleasant conversation.

They stand next to each other, by the rail.

"We won't be disturbed," says Alejandro. Sheldon wants to look around, to see what or who Bernal has employed to guard the door, but decides to affect good ol' boy nonchalance. He sips his beer.

"Bad day at the office," says Alejandro.

It's not clear whether he is speaking of himself or of Sheldon, but Sheldon has been in enough of these conversations to know that answering in any form will be an invitation to be ignored, an opening for Bernal to affect some wild non sequitur, just for the pleasure of displaying that this exchange is his plaything, and not an equal conversation.

"We're not very happy, as you can imagine," adds Bernal.

The point reached, Sheldon replies. "Steve Carter's homophobic rant or the review snafu or just this whole business with the rogue blogger? Take your pick Alejandro. Because I'm not real happy either."

"It's the review, of course," says Bernal. "Not just the libel, but the gross mishandling that came afterwards."

They stand apart from the rail now, face each other.

"I made an error," replies Sheldon.

"Then again, it's the fact that I was in your offices a few weeks ago, and it turns out," Bernal laughs, "it turns out that one of your scribblers has been bugging meetings, and may, or may not, have something damning to offer the world. Another error?"

He looks around with comic urgency, searching the bare balcony floor. "How the hell do I know I'm not being bugged now?"

"It's in hand."

"Like the thing with the robot?" Bernal smiles. "Yes, I heard about your editor, chasing Claptrap across an industry party floor. I mean, seriously Sheldon, what kind of retards are you people?"

Bernal holds his hand up, an imperious demand for silence. Sheldon feels a powerful urge to smash his beer bottle over this fucker's face, but seeks to save face, to curb his rage, by turning away, gazing down at all the people in the street, having fun, not being harangued and humiliated.

"As for Steve Carter, well, he's a fool, just one of about a dozen little halfwits you've decided to hire because they're cheap and malleable, until they go haywire, of course."

Sheldon has no argument with this line of reasoning.

"Here's the thing. I know how to run a business," says Bernal. "Hire good people. Know your craft. Set clear goals. All that stuff. You, Sheldon. You don't. This is why you are in this mess. None of this concerns me, except your stink, the stink of your shitty incompetence, is heading my way. And this is a problem."

Sheldon turns back, makes a shrugging motion, a look of regret, as if the weather had turned out unexpectedly inclement. He has no intention of groveling now, because he knows, without any doubt, what's coming next.

"Just tell me what you want to do, Bernal," he says. This use of the surname is his only affectation of machismo nonchalance, and he can see its transparency, the dismal failure of its intended effect, from the patronizing smile on the other man's face.

Now Bernal approaches Sheldon, puts his arm around his shoulders, speaks softly, almost friendly "We're pulling all marketing support," he says. "We're disconnecting all PR support, all links between Saturnine and Piranha Frenzy, effective immediately."

"I see," says Sheldon. Before he can shake himself free, Bernal pats him on the back and walks away.

"When you get your house in order, we can talk again, I'm sure."

"We'll survive, I guess," says Sheldon, calculating just how far adrift of their target they are going to be, and what this will mean in terms of lost bonuses, executive firings and newsroom redundancies.

"One more thing," says Bernal. "If I'm on that video tomorrow, if I have been secretly filmed by one of your employees, you'll be hearing from our lawyers. It's going to get ugly, Sheldon."

Sheldon nods. There is nothing else he can do.

"Now," Bernal checks his watch. "I'm going to go in and watch my beautiful girlfriend, the only good thing to come out of your disgusting little enterprise, give her little welcome speech and then I'm going to have dinner with some friends."

Sheldon watches him leave the balcony. He turns back to L.A. Live, toys briefly with returning to the time travel fantasy, but it's gone. He finishes his beer and heads back into the party. He too wants to hear what Kjersti Wong has to say.

18

THE CANTINA BAND

8:25 p.m.

Gingerly, the alien man makes his way down the stage's five side steps, removes a very large, bulbous head costume and runs a hand through his long hair, sweat beads all over his face.

Kjersti recalls his name is Martin, the trumpeter from a sci-fi jazz quartet called These Aren't the Droids, a regular fixture at game industry parties, always dressed up as the Mos Eisley Cantina band.

"Hi, Kjersti," he says, leaning down toward her. "I just gotta few seconds here. The plan is, we'll play our theme, and then you just come on up and do your thing. When we think you're done, we'll go straight into the Supergirl Overture."

She frowns at this, the cramping nerves she feels at this impending speech are invading and corrupting all her social signals.

"Too cheesy?" he asks, genuinely concerned.

"Way too cheesy," she says. "I love it." But she doesn't love it. She's about to quit. Supergirl is all wrong. They should be playing the Imperial Death March.

"OK." And he's back up the steps, replacing his head, complete with special trumpet hole. The Cantina song begins.

An audible wave of appreciation sweeps the room, dozens of conversations dip into the shared cultural pit that is Star Wars. Jokes and impressions abound.

She feels it as a lump in her throat: suddenly, this sense of belonging, this knowledge that she has found her place in the great confusion of Planet Earth 2016.

The game industry, the coolest nerds on earth, the people most effortlessly comfortable with their own cultural obsessions. This sci-fi jazz-riff is their Ode to Joy, their Stompin' at the Savoy, their Jimmy Hendrix playing the The Star Spangled Banner. It's the anthem that binds them together.

"Piranha Frenzy is the biggest audience you'll ever have." The words have been with her since her conversation with Liam at the LACC coffee booth. "Today's video show you recorded, the one you phoned in because you've done it a million times before, you'll spend the rest of your life trying to get back there, to get back to an audience that big, and you might not make it."

She'd told him about her resolve to quit. It had all come out, this crazy idea of Alex's to launch a new game website, to be an EIC, to create game journalism the way she wants it to be. She was making it up as she went along, filling in the gaps that were opening up even as she grasped what it would mean for her to actually walk out.

Liam had sat quietly, sipped his Americana.

His point about audience size was a good one. "I know," she'd said. "But where else do I go? What can I do?" She'd thought about Frank, trudging out of the office, the photo of his wife under his arm, his old dictionaries in a box.

He shrugged. "I came to Piranha Frenzy because, yeah, I wanted to work with you, truly. So I'm disappointed. But also because I'm greedy for audience, and Piranha Frenzy has the biggest. If you're the same, you're gonna miss them—the big, big numbers I mean."

"It's not enough for me," she'd said. "Maybe when I was your age—I don't want to be patronizing but it's true—when I was younger I lived for the big audience. But now, I feel like a sham. This character," she pointed at herself, with both hands, a gesture of derision, "it's not me, not anymore."

"I get it; it's probably the right move. But you'll miss it. That's all I'm saying. This new thing. It's going to be small, for a very long time, maybe forever. You're a somebody right now, because of the audience. But tomorrow?"

Now, at the G2G party, waiting to give her traditional welcome speech, standing at the bottom of the stage steps, she hears the Cantina song coming to an end, starts to make her way up toward the mic stand. She's spoken on stages to large groups of people many times before and hasn't suffered from nerves in years, but this time her legs are shaking and her mouth is dry.

Liam had said, "You're doing the welcome speech tonight, at the party. What are you going to say?"

And so she had given him an extemporized 30-second speech, about how game journalism has been corrupted by outdated practices, by an old-boys network determined to maintain their own place of privilege, by a hegemony of middle-aged white males who no longer represented gaming, if they ever really had. She was going to move on and reinvent game journalism for the gamers of twenty-first century. For everyone. Thank you very much.

The music stops and she's at the mic, just about everyone is facing her, the clapping, the smiles, they are all looking at her. But there are some people who are not smiling. She sees Sheldon, leaning against a far wall. Brad looking at his shoes. Steve, drinking and frowning. Alejandro, arms folded, expectant. She looks for Frank and remembers why he is not there. Liam is there too, watchful.

In the cafeteria Liam had greeted her speech with a raised eyebrow, and given her a strong "I'm saying nothing" signal.

"What?" she'd asked.

He tipped his head slightly, as if knocking a stray bee with his temple.

"It's all true," he said. "It's noble and right."

"But…"

He looked at his coffee. "Who are you, Kjersti—to them, I mean?"

"You tell me."

"You're something different from the Steve Carters of this world. You're not cynical. You're not angry. People, they like you."

"And they won't like me if I give that speech?"

"Not one bit."

"You're assuming that being liked is the most important thing for me." There was an edge in her voice. She was annoyed. "Is it for you, Liam?"

He took a moment to answer. "It's important to me, yes. It allows me to be accepted so I do the work I want to do. It's just the way the world is. You're angry and bitter right now, but that doesn't mean you're an angry and bitter person."

On stage, she has waited a second too long to begin speaking, the clapping is coming to an end, the smiles she sees are beginning to take on a slightly frozen aspect.

She can name almost every person in the audience, many of them people she has worked with for years. They have a view of her, just as Liam said, that she's about to trash. The video of this speech will be on YouTube in minutes. There will be outrage, she knows.

She looks at Alejandro, a hint of concern in his face. She realizes she is not smiling. The smiles in the crowd are slipping away.

"It's important," Alejandro had said in their meeting. "It's essential that you reinvent yourself, that you leave the old Kjersti Wong behind. She is the enemy now. She is too much Piranha Frenzy. And you are in a fight with her that will go to the death."

"The knife," he'd said. "You need to strike true."

She must talk, now. The silence is deathly.

19

EPIPHANY

8:38 p.m.

When it's over, when the Supergirl theme begins, she climbs down from the stage. They come to her in large groups, congrats and kisses, "We'll miss you" and declarations of love and admiration. There is clapping and smiling and as the applause fades she spends what seems like an age working her way toward an exit.

She finds a pillar, leans against it, she wants the ordeal to be over. She tries Frank's phone, yet again. Sends him another text. She's worried.

"So, you changed your mind," says Liam, smiling at her.

"You were right," she replies, semi-searching the room for Sheldon, who she want to avoid. "It seemed wrong to stand up there and rant."

"Still, you managed to get a few jabs in about your review. I can't imagine the bosses will be very happy."

"Yeah," she says. "I can live without seeing Sheldon or Brad right now. I'd better skip town while I can."

"Fair enough," he says. "If I know YouTube, and I think I do, your speech will get a lot of views."

She thanks him, says she's sorry they won't get to work together.

"One last piece of advice?" she says, before leaving. "Be careful who you trust here. It might be all Star Wars figures and MMO marathons, but it's still an office."

"You going to tell me to just be myself?" he laughs. "Go on, get lost. And good luck."

They embrace and she makes for the exit. Now that her time as the party's center of attention has definitely passed, she finds it easier to slip through the throng of bodies.

A text arrives, from Alejandro.

Dinner is at 9:15. Don't be late. Important people.

Near the end of her speech, she had seen Alejandro making his way to the exit. He needed to be at the restaurant in good time for her guests, she tells herself.

A follow-up text arrives from him. She thinks, "He'll say something supportive now, he'll say that I handled it right, that everything is going to turn out great."

They don't like to be disappointed

Disappointed.

She'd begun the speech by saying that, as a youngster, all she'd wanted was to work in game journalism, that it had been a wonderful privilege to work with such an amazing group of people, that fronting the world's most successful game website had been a life-changing experience.

But it was time to move on. She was angry, it was true, by the day's events. Her managers had made an error, and she hoped they would find a way to correct their mistake. She stood by her review even though, she acknowledged, it would have been better to be able to produce some evidence of her memories.

It was also true that she found some of the messages coming out of the organization, some of the casual frat-boy homophobia and sexism, dispiriting.

And she believed that criticisms of game journalism's cozy relationship with game publishers was probably a cause for valid concern. That said, she was in no position to cast aspersions where cozy relationships were concerned. This had gotten a good laugh. From the back of the room, Alejandro had half-heartedly raised his glass to her.

She's in the stairwell. A nifty escape, she thinks. Sheldon successfully avoided, or perhaps he had chosen to ignore her. During her speech, he had stood in the shadows.

Sheldon has been known to blank former employees after they have departed for new projects, except of course, for the ones who have gone into marketing, who have landed budgets or access to exclusives.

Kjersti wants to take the stairs two or three at a time, but she's wearing heels. She can just about walk to the restaurant and make it in good time, but she needs to see Alejandro first, alone. She wants to explain that she couldn't twist the knife, that it just wasn't in her.

Concluding her speech, she'd told them that she would be launching her own media outlet, not because she was hell-bent on destroying Piranha Frenzy, but because she wanted to have her own voice; because the things she wanted to say, and the way she wanted to say them could not be accommodated at an outlet like Piranha Frenzy.

The implication that Piranha Frenzy has become a storefront for marketing assets, sycophancy and sophomoric diatribes hung in the air.

She'd finished with some more words of praise for selected colleagues, most especially for Frank who "can't be here tonight."

That's when she'd seen Alejandro leave. Disappointed.

She opens the exit door onto a dumpster alleyway at the side of the restaurant, turns toward the street, enjoys the sensation of cool air, the promise of anonymity among the crowds.

Sheldon steps into her path.

"We need to talk," he says.

Sheldon is a large man, almost wide enough to fill the entrance to the alleyway. Kjersti won't allow him to block her path to the street. She steps past him, before turning to speak.

"I'm late for dinner, Sheldon. I'm sorry. I can't stop."

"I'll walk with you," he says. "I really just want to say a few words."

A group of young G2G people pass them, bouncing off another, laughing.

"OK, let's walk," she says.

"I told you earlier that you could achieve great things with us," he says, heaving slightly at the effort of walking beside her.

She knows she should slow her walk to his pace. But she does not want to be late. Alejandro and his friends will be there, enjoying cocktails, mingling with one another. He counts, among his friends, leading creatives, execs and investors, the most powerful people in the video game industry.

"I remember the conversation," she says.

"I... I have made mistakes, Kjersti. Like you said in the speech. I know I've screwed this all up. The review. But we couldn't let it stand. Not without evidence."

She stops. "The review? That's what you think I'm angry about? Fuck the review. You fired my best friend in the world today. Because... Why?"

"That's just business. Numbers. I'm talking about something bigger here, about our direction. I guess I'm having an epiphany."

"Are you serious, Sheldon? You've thrown a good man like Frank into the trash, but somehow this is all about you?"

"It's been today, all of it. Steve behaving like such an asshole, the whole thing with the Scourge and then your review. It's just brought everything into focus for me."

She has never heard Sheldon, or anyone in authority at Piranha Frenzy, speak this way. She reminds herself that Sheldon is in a tight corner, and, in her experience, bosses in a fix are shameless liars.

He stops and stands in front of her. She sees he is taking up too much of the sidewalk, forcing groups of people into the road to pass them. She has to stand close to him. She smells beer on his breath.

"I know we have to make changes. I want you to take some time to think about your next move. This is a bad time to be launching a new game website. I've seen a lot of people disappear."

"I'm moving on. There's nothing for me here."

"The culture has to change. I know that. Things are going to be different."

"Like how?" she asks. They're at a street corner, near the restaurant. Taxis roll past.

"Specifics?" He shrugs. "It's too soon. It needs thought. But we'll get there. You can get beyond what happened today and be a part of this."

She looks toward the restaurant, to see if he's waiting outside. It's a nonsensical notion. He'll be with the investors, yukking it up, exchanging their old-boy-network jokes.

"You called me a cunt," she says quietly, looking directly at him.

He looks deflated. "That was before..."

"Your great epiphany?"

Her phone rings. She looks at the screen. Frank's name.

"This new thing of yours? It's small-fry," Sheldon says. "Don't let pride get in the way. I'm offering you something that can last."

But she's already on the phone, talking to Frank, walking away.

20

STREETS OF RAGE

9:12 p.m.

"Frank? What's up? I've been calling you for hours."

"I'm drinking."

"Oh, Frank. Jesus. Shouldn't you call your sponsor?"

" ..."

"Frank?"

"Yes. Yes. I probably should. But... I... I want to talk to you, Kjersti."

He's been dry for six months now. Back in the day, the two of them had spent many hours in bars and restaurants enjoying each other's company, laughing and quaffing. He'd generally managed to get to a state of inebriation that seemed controlled.

But when his wife, diagnosed with muscular dystrophy, lost her mobility, his drinking took on a darker edge. He'd finish work and go to a bar and drink alone. He stopped socializing. He'd arrive at work late, shabby and smelling of booze. He became irritable, withdrawn.

One night he called Kjersti, weeping. He'd been picked up by the police, walking in a busy road without his pants on. It was the sort of tale that might have made a funny story in the faded alcohol-machismo culture of old-school journalism in which he had been raised.

Frank had counted on the fact that Kjersti would never see anything funny about it at all. He needed help. She fetched him, told him that he knew what to do next. He'd agreed, his face puffed with booze, humiliation and sorrow. He joined a program the next day.

"Where are you?"

"Er. ... What's the name of this dump, pal? ... Ah... The Watering Hole on South Flower? Yeah, South Flower... Are you at the party?" He is slurring.

She recalls the first time they met: 2006, the year of Hot Coffee, *Oblivion, Okami, Gears of War, Twilight Princess*, the arrival of Wii and PlayStation 3. It was her first year in game journalism.

He'd been distant at first, having little to do with the recently formed video team. She had been busy learning how to talk to camera, refining her style, always staying ahead of events, playing every game she could, because, even then—especially then— there were many who scorned her as a pretty thing placed in front of the camera to read lines she could not possibly comprehend.

"The party? I just left," she says. "On my way to dinner with Alejandro."

"Oh. Well, never mind then. It'll wait."

The bosses, Sheldon in fact, had feared a cultural schism between the entrenched editorial team and the new video team, and there'd been one of those semi-regular desk moves, this one designed to merge the teams.

Kjersti had been placed directly opposite Frank, perhaps some sort of a joke on Frank who they might have seen as a stuffy old fart for whom the presence of a female in the editorial office might cause ink-bottle spillage and quill set aflutter.

"Go home, Frank," she says.

"Yeah. I should do that. Maybe later. Been a bad day, y'know? End of the line and all that."

"Come on, Frank. This won't help."

Back in '06, Piranha Frenzy had never before hired a full-time female writer, and only rarely used female freelancers. He'd shown an interest in her work, had known of and been impressed with the writing she'd previously done in Norway and Scotland. He had asked her to submit some articles, had helped tighten her writing style, had warned her off the most egregious crimes against language, encouraged her to experiment and to be playful.

Kjersti has friends in the office, work friends. But Frank had become the closest thing she had to a real friend.

"I'll see you later, Kjersti," he says. "Maybe grab a coffee once the dust settles. I'm sure it'll all be fine."

"Oh, Frank."

"It'll be fine. Really. You go on."

"..."

"Kjersti?"

"..."

"Hello, are you there, Kjersti?"

"Fuck it, Frank. Stay where you are. I'll be with you in ten minutes."

21

A 2001 POWERBOOK G4

9:13 p.m.

Sheldon Tavernier has been around media crises long enough to know that if you aren't the one lopping off noggins, you might just be the one being decapitated.

After Kjersti turns her back on him and walks away, Sheldon stands on the curb for at least a minute, wondering if his career is about to permadeath.

He has no doubt that the combination of Kjersti's unexpected departure, the Steve Carter and *Satanic Realm 5* debacles, Saturnine pulling its ad campaign and whatever this Charlie Black video might reveal, will result in the spectacle of rolling heads.

Standing earlier on that balcony outside the party, standing there in the aftermath of the humiliation piled upon him by Alejandro Bernal, Sheldon had decided that there would need to be a clear-out of bodies, one designed to portray Piranha Frenzy as reacting aggressively, a progressive, slightly edgy organization.

His reaction to all this clusterfuckery, he decides, will need to be a collective act of contrition, a grave acceptance that change had come and that Piranha Frenzy would welcome its responsibility to be part of that change. He might even get away with pitching the whole thing as integral to a long-desired strategic initiative.

Brad might well serve as a useful and unproblematic sacrifice. Steve might be more of a tangled knot. Whatever the details, they were part of the old narrative. Fresh faces—a fresh start—is required.

Sheldon knows he is the most vulnerable of them all, the most identifiable with the past. He thinks about the twentieth anniversary planned for the morning, the celebration of an era, he now sees, that is finished. He will make what use of that he can.

Firing people will help him look strong. But people quitting looks bad. He needs Kjersti to stick around, at least for a while, while he punches through the membrane that separates the past from the future.

He knows that whatever she is planning to do next is provisional upon her overcoming obstacles she has not yet comprehended. There are other barriers that Sheldon, given an opportunity, will be happy to throw in her way.

He will find a way to stand before the gaming world and insist that everything is going to be different, that the power brokers and back-room deals are a thing of the past. Sheldon will appear to be suitably humbled, a man evolved.

But there's another task he needs to undertake right now, to mitigate the unfolding disaster.

He slips his cell phone from a pocket and autodials a number.

"Brad. You still at the party?"

He nods at the expected affirmation.

"Sober enough to drive? ... Good. Come and get me now. I'm in front of a restaurant called The Fancy Duck... Yes, the one on the corner... Don't worry about why, just get here... We have a job to do that might well save your job."

Fifteen minutes later they're on the 5 headed for Culver City.

"We need to get to Charlie and persuade him that it's not in his best interest to release that film," says Sheldon, shifting uncomfortably in the cramped passenger seat of a Camry, finally answering Brad's inquiry as to why they are going to Charlie's house.

"Do you think he'd really kill the video?"

"Hell if I know. But I'm not going to wait for it to come out without talking to the little prick."

"Why would Charlie do this to us?" Brad is rubbing the mark above his eye, where Claptrap's flailing hand had caught him a few hours before.

But Sheldon is looking out of the window now, trying to think through the permutations. The "why" of Charlie doesn't interest him. What he needs to know is what Charlie will take as payment for killing that video. Everyone, after all, has a price.

They arrive at the house, its location still in Brad's GPS from the weird barbecue Charlie had hosted a few weeks back.

Sheldon remembers the party, a strange little affair. Charlie had behaved like some rube throwing his first small-town BBQ. It had been a gathering of unironic crassness, the music neither old enough to be deemed nostalgic, nor new enough to be fashionable.

Charlie had darted about serving sliders and premade Margaritas with the delight of someone who believed no one could possibly have imagined such glamour before.

The house is a small 1940s suburban affair in a dreary neighborhood, not much changed since it was built. There are no lights on. They try ringing an old-fashioned bell, they knock on the door.

"He's not home," says Brad. "Shall I try his cell?"

"No," says Sheldon. "We'll wait."

"Wait?" Brad holds his hands out. "He could be hours. It's past 10. There are a dozen G2G parties on tonight."

Sheldon looks at him, decides that if he announces Brad's firing straight after the release of the video, it might be enough of a smokescreen for him to make his next move; it might buy him a little time.

"He's not partying. Let's see if we can go inside and wait."

"That's not cool, not cool at all," says Brad, his voice inching upwards toward the alarmed-and-nervous range.

"It's fine. You never seen a noir movie? We wait inside."

He heads around the back, tries the rear door. Looks under the doormat. There's a key.

"Jesus Christ. What a doofus," he whispers, opening the door slowly, just in case there's an alarm. "Anyone in? Charlie, you here?"

Brad is still on the back doorstep, shaking his head. "Not cool, man."

"Get in here," hisses Sheldon. And then, as he sees Brad step reluctantly over the threshold, he adds more soothingly, "No need to turn on the lights. Don't want him driving up and freaking out."

They're in the house, moving through the kitchen, into the living room at the front of the house. The sound of a car outside stills both men, just for a moment. Brad checks the curtains to see if Charlie has arrived outside, but it's just someone driving by.

Sheldon surveys the room. There's no furniture. He remembers this from the party, but thought then that it had merely been moved to make room for the guests. There's only a PowerBook G4 from maybe 2001 on a table next to an old video camera and a cell phone.

He turns on the laptop; it's just in sleep mode. It opens onto some ancient Apple video editing software. There's a paused image at the center of the editing suite. It takes Sheldon a few moments to comprehend that the image is of the back of his own head.

"It's the footage from the party. The Claptrap stuff. He's been back here and uploaded it already."

Brad looks out to the driveway again. "He must have just gone out to get something. We should go."

"Are you not getting this Brad? This is the final edit, and all his gear. We take this, the movie goes away. Quick, check upstairs for any hard drives, memory sticks, anything."

"He might have it saved on a cloud," Brad says, but Sheldon is already gathering up the computer.

"My guess is that it's all right here," says Sheldon, yanking a power cable out of the machine. "My guess is that Charlie Black doesn't trust any kind of cloud."

Brad hesitates a moment, then leaves the room to search upstairs. Sheldon begins rifling around for any data devices.

After a few moments, Brad returns, shaking his head, checking the window once again. "There's nothing up there except a bed and a few clothes."

"Good. You grab the laptop. Let's get out of here."

"Hold on. No, I'm not burglarizing the dude. That's criminal."

Sheldon carries on gathering up the gear, suppresses an urge to curse at Brad. "He's been filming us in secret. We're within our rights. Now let's do this. Or do you want to watch yourself being humiliated all over YouTube tomorrow?"

Sheldon grabs the camera and the phone, unplugs it from the PowerBook. After a pause, Brad helps, lifts up the antique computer.

Within a few minutes the table is clear and every piece of electronic gear in Charlie's house is in the trunk of Brad's Camry. Sheldon climbs into the passenger seat. He hasn't moved so fast in years. He's panting, sweating.

When they get onto the freeway, again he checks the time. It's just past 10:30 p.m. "Can you drop me home, Brad, maybe go on and get rid of this stuff?"

Brad looks over, shakes his head, but Sheldon knows Brad will do as he's told. "OK, let's see this movie," he chuckles. "A little sneak preview."

He switches on the PowerBook and begins the film. The heading comes up, white text on a black background, some standard crappy Mac text thing: "The ROTTEN CORRUPTION at the Heart of Video Game Reviews, a film by Lars Roby."

Sheldon frowns at this. The screen goes black again... "aka Charlie Black, formerly Piranha Frenzy news editor, undercover investigator."

"Charlie..." Sheldon shouts. "Charlie is related to Roby, he must be... Roby's son. It's incredible. He's embedded his own son with us just to fuck me. Sweet Jesus."

The film is just a few minutes long. The party footage has been thrown in at the end, but has not been edited completely.

Sheldon switches off the laptop.

"That's it," he says to Brad. "Did you hear all that?"

"Pretty much," says Brad.

"There's nothing here. Just a bunch of bad camera shots, some incoherent recordings and Charlie sounding like a paranoid nutcase, like the unholy spawn of Don Roby." He laughs. "This is the crappiest thing I've ever seen. It's terrible."

"Isn't that, like, good news?"

"This is great news, Brad. Roby's going to be a laughing stock. How long has Charlie been watching us? And this is it?"

Brad's relief is physical. He slumps slightly in his chair.

Sheldon laughs again, but only for a moment. "Tell no one about this, Brad. Not ever. We burgled Charlie—Lars Roby, whatever he's called—and we'll go to jail if we're caught. Get rid of the GPS, all this shit, don't leave a single scrap of evidence. When they ask where we were, you took me home and then you went straight back to your place and then you went to bed. Just figure out the timings from when you picked me up at the restaurant. Got it?"

"Got it."

"I think I'm going to sleep a touch easier tonight. The Scourge of Corruption. Don-fucking-Roby and his crazy boy." He starts to laugh again. "Those losers."

22

MS. PAC-MAN

9:27 p.m.

"What shall we drink to?"

Frank isn't exactly slurring, but he doesn't seem entirely steady on his barstool. He looks at her, a wonky smile of self-mockery. He turns his attention back to a glass of whisky.

"Is there any point in me telling you to leave that off and to go home?" she asks, nodding at the drink.

"Up your arse, Vicky the Viking," he says, laughs, drains his glass and seeks out the bartender.

A basketball game is running on the television, glum patrons slouch at the bar, gaze at the screens, mostly alone.

"Let's talk, just for a while. I'll have one drink," she says. "Then you'll bugger-off home?"

"Sure. Sure."

Frank ignores her. He seems to have forgotten that he is the one who called her and asked her to join him. He has also forgotten that this intervention is keeping her away from a dinner engagement. More probably, he's dismissed it as some unessential pre-G2G glad-handing thing. Kjersti reminds herself that he's got his own ruined career to think about, his own lack of acceptable options.

Alejandro will have to deal with the investors on his own. They won't be happy that she's skipped the meeting. They will be disappointed. That word again.

She orders a beer, texts Alejandro.

Frank in trouble. Sorry. Gotta help him. Pass on apols plz

"I'm sorry," she says to Frank. "About today. You don't deserve that."

"I do though," he says, his eyes on the basketball game. "I'm old and irrelevant. I took the easy option and opted for game journalism...," he says, placing sarcastic finger quotes around these last two words, "...instead of real journalism. I deserve it because I just couldn't smile and nod when Sheldon and Brad flapped their gums."

She sips her beer.

"I quit Piranha Frenzy," she says. "Just now. I told Sheldon to go fuck himself, or words to that effect."

He turns and gapes at her. "Not for me. Please say it wasn't about me." He looks pained, almost pleading, his face is red and his eyes are dim.

"It didn't help that they did that to you, Frank," she says. "But I couldn't stay. Not after they killed my review."

Frank takes a drink. She wants him to slow down. She's tempted to say something, but keeps her mouth shut. She'll let it pass, bundle him into a cab first chance she gets, deliver him home to his wife.

Her phone buzzes. A text from Alejandro.

Are you kidding me? Forget Frank. This is important.

She hopes Frank will go home, wake up tomorrow and call his sponsor, maybe start going to meetings again. Then again, unemployment at an advanced age is rarely an opportunity for life improvement.

"Sheldon's having a bad day too, I suppose," he says.

"I came here to talk about you."

"I won't miss them," he says. "They treat me like I'm a retro museum piece. Like I'm the Fonz or something, another one of their cool little dolls."

"You think of me like that?"

He looks at her, his eyes wavering. "Nah. You're different, Kjersti. You're the only one who was my friend."

"Is your friend," she corrects him.

"Those yapping puppies," he says, gulping his drink, finishing it.

"That's not fair," she says. "They respect you."

He ignores this. "You helped me, Kjersti; you helped me when I really needed it." He tips the glass toward her. "And this is how I repay you."

"I'm here to help you again," she says, carefully negotiating a conversation that she can see is veering toward disaster. "We're friends, remember? Let me take you home."

He turns away, orders another drink. She sees that he is stuck in a treacle of self-pity; she knows there is no way for her to pull him free. She changes the subject, says, "I'm thinking about setting up my own thing. Just something small."

He looks at her briefly, but his face is blank. Frank, who had always claimed that journalism is all about taking an interest in the lives of others, cannot see beyond his own misery.

A group of four young men pour into the bar, jolly and flushed with alcohol, obviously out-of-towners gallivanting in L.A.'s glamour. The bartender serves them without enthusiasm. They are wearing retro-gaming T-shirts.

"Hey, it's Kjersti Wong. Kjersti!" She looks up to see them gather their drinks and approach her. A moment of panic passes through her, that they might be yet more *Satanic Realm 5* fans come to hate on her. But they are friendly. They are fans. She greets them. Frank turns his back.

She tries to be friendly and chitchats about the games they are most excited about seeing at G2G. They gabble about the big new games at the show. No one mentions *Satanic Realm 5*.

She's about to politely dismiss them when Frank turns to them, raises a glass. "Who here is interested in working as a game journalist?" He's slurring.

They are guarded about this drunken old man, but they reply with assent and joking. It sounds like a better job than the dull work they do. One of them is a prison guard, another works in a call center.

Kjersti introduces Frank as the long-standing managing editor of Piranha Frenzy and a man who knows everything worth knowing about the game industry. The young men greet him warmly. "Old school," says one of them.

Frank takes a long sip of his drink, puts his hand up for another, but one of the young men is already at the bar, saying he'll get this.

"It's the most wonderful job in the world," says Frank. "Getting paid to play video games. Getting paid to write about them. Wonderful."

He takes the drink. Looks at it long and hard before downing it.

"What I can't understand is why so many people who do it seem to be so unhappy," he says.

He steps down from his chair, wobbles as the men step back. Kjersti steadies him.

For a moment, she sees Frank's fate unfolding before her, the bitter drunk banging on about something no one cares about, latching onto any poor saloon dweller who expresses the slightest interest in video games. Here is his sad little speech, destined to be repeated again and again.

"We live on a planet that supports several thousand people who write about video games," he says. "That is incredible, isn't it?"

Kjersti pulls a face to the lads that her friend has had too much to drink. They nod; they spot an arcade machine and head over to the game. It's *Ms. Pac-Man*.

Once they are out of earshot, she says, "What the hell was that all about, Frank?"

"Your audience," says Frank, gesturing loosely toward them. "You reckon they'll come with you to the new thing you're doing?"

He leans against the bar, catches his breath, his head hanging. He looks up for the bartender, but she grabs his arm, directs him to look at her.

"Please. Let's go home."

"I blame those fuckers—the audience," he says, his voice rising. "They're all experts aren't they? With their blogs and their podcasts and their fucking opinions."

"It's not that simple," she says. "Maybe, maybe we can go someplace else?"

"They're killing us."

"We're surviving."

He looks at her. "Are we?"

"Sorry," she says. "That was stupid of me."

Another text buzzes from Alejandro.

It's now or never. Don't blow this

After a pause, she says, "You're still valuable Frank. Quality counts."

"Sophistry and horseshit."

"Come on," she says. "Let me get you home."

He looks at her. "I've seen a lot of people go it alone, Kjersti. Most of them disappear."

She smiles. "What d'you suggest. That I stay and pitch in with Sheldon?" She's guiding him toward the door.

"Naw. You do what you want to do." He stands up straight, slowly, turns to the guys playing *Ms. Pac-Man*. "Fellas," he declares grandly. "This is Kjersti Wong. The future of game journalism."

A wary, forced round of applause.

She smiles, affects a mock bow. Frank staggers. She holds him up, helps him toward the door.

Her phone buzzes again. It's Alejandro. She reads the text while helping Frank through the door.

Your moment's gone.

It takes a few minutes to flag down a cab and bundle Frank into the back seat. He's just about able to articulate his address, she climbs in and soon they are on the freeway, crawling through traffic. A quiet settles upon them.

Lolling his head against the cab window, Frank seems to sleep, but then he murmurs to himself. "My wife won't be happy." His usual fierce quickness, she thinks, is now engulfed in his own drunken unhappiness.

Kjersti looks out of her side window, wonders how long this interminable ride will last. She suffers pinpricks of shame, wondering too how long her friendship with Frank has to run, now that they no longer share the experience of working together, now that their convenient office-political alliance has been broken by his fall.

It bothers her now, angers her, this idea that she came to her friend's aid tonight.

Even though it was the right thing to do, it was also the wrong thing. In the years ahead, how many times will she see Frank? How many genuinely open conversations will they have? The man has never invited Kjersti into his house, has never even introduced her to his wife, rarely talks about her.

Yes, he is my friend, but I have done this, she decides, to make myself feel like a good human being. Worse, I have done this to avoid facing Alejandro's big shot pals, schmoozing them with the sleazy patois of the game industry supplicant.

As much as she wants what they have to offer—a news outlet all of her own, to shape as she sees fit—the notion of sucking up to these people terrifies her. She ducked the meeting because, deep down, she doesn't want to deal with those people.

At last, the cab rolls up to Frank's condo. He turns and holds her hand. Thanks her and stumbles out of the cab. Kjersti watches as he fumbles with his keys and lets himself in. She looks at the red lights of the cab fare, sighs, and directs the driver to her home address.

She looks at Alejandro's text again. "Your moment's gone."

The tone of it angers her, and she feels her mind swirling in tighter and tighter circles toward the inevitable self-recriminations.

And she remembers something else. Alejandro, full of directions about how she ought to behave, what kind of resignation speech she ought to give, who she ought to meet, he still hasn't been straight with her about the review. She decides now that he lied to her about *Dare You Enter the Devil's Lair?*.

"I've changed my mind," she says to the driver. She tells him the address of Alejandro's downtown apartment.

23

THE TRUTH

11.48 p.m.

"I told you. Our mission is the truth. I am the weapon. I am the mission. I am the truth."

The incredibly loud voice she hears is Master Chief. She is standing in the corridor outside Alejandro's apartment, knocking on his door. Alejandro is home, playing the new Halo game. The game's audio dissolves into rapid gunfire and alien death squawks.

Knocking is a waste of time. She reaches into her bag, finds her keys.

Alejandro's real home is in Huntington Beach, a beachfront place she has only visited a few times. Mostly, they hang out here, in the downtown apartment owned by Saturnine and used ostensibly to house visiting bigwigs or to host media demos. It's under the marketing department's aegis and so has become Alejandro's pad. He gave her a key weeks ago. She has stayed here maybe a dozen times, enjoying the luxury of privacy, a discreet place absent an infestation of noisy housemates.

She has become accustomed here, of trying not to think too hard about the ethical labyrinth her relationship has created. This part of her relationship with Alejandro she has not shared with anyone else, not even Frank. The reactions that might greet such an arrangement are all too easy to imagine.

Opening the door to the apartment, she walks through a corridor past a small kitchen. In the living room, the game is running by itself, an Xbox One controller has been tossed onto the sofa. Master Chief's perspective shows that he is crouching behind a mauve vehicle, the battle rages noisily. Soon he will be found and killed.

"Alex," she calls out, and walks toward the main bedroom door. It is slightly ajar. "Alejandro."

The aliens have surrounded Master Chief. She can hear him being slain, can hear the grim music that greets failure. As it lilts away from the clatter of carnage, as it slides into elegy, she hears Alejandro's voice from inside the bedroom, and she stops to listen.

"Good, good," he says. "And it's the only one? You're sure?"

There is a pause. She knows she shouldn't be eavesdropping. She steps back; perhaps she should go to the kitchen and put on a pot of coffee or something, an activity of innocence.

"Don't worry about that. I'll take care of her," he says. "Just make sure I get it by tomorrow. OK?"

The conversation is ending. She scuttles back to the kitchen. By the time he emerges from the bedroom, sees her and registers surprise and dismay, she has a bottle of Merlot and a bottle opener in her shaking hands and she is making much of the business at hand.

"Oh, hey," she says. "Loud, isn't it?" she nods toward the game. Using a voice command, he switches off the game. The TV blinks into a news broadcast, blaring talk about politicians. He turns the volume down.

She had wanted to come here and confront him, but now she feels like a thief and an intruder. Even as the bottle opens and she attends to finding some glasses the certainty is in her mind, that she is the "her" in his phone conversation.

"I didn't expect to see you tonight," he says.

"My housemates were all getting high and being annoying," she lies. "And anyway, I wanted to talk to you, about tonight."

He takes the glass she offers him. "I'm glad," he says, smiling at her before taking a sip. "Best not to go to bed with bad feelings. Mmmm, this is pretty good."

He looks at her, presents himself, as if to say, "Let's get this out of the way."

"So, tonight..." he says.

She can almost feel the words "I'm sorry" forming on her lips, rising from deep within her, the need to make amends for her absence from his meeting, but instead, she stares at him and shrugs.

"The guys," he says. "They're not going to back you. Maybe if you'd given a different speech, something with backbone, maybe if you'd come to the meeting... But that's all speculation. It's all in the past."

She fills her glass again. "Uh-huh," she says.

"I'm sorry if my texts were a little terse," he says. "Some things are just not meant to be, and we should move on from this episode."

He waits for her to respond. She watches him over the rim of her wineglass.

"So, it's fine," he says. "You've got so much talent, we don't need them. I've had another idea."

"I'll take care of her," he'd said on the phone. And she thinks about how he had ducked her allegations of plagiarism when they had talked at LACC and how on earth she is going to ask him about that now, and what the "it" is he'd talked about and wanted delivered, and she wonders if none of it has anything to do with her and if she's just being paranoid, and she's out of work and facing a one-way trip back to Bergen and she hasn't slept for two days.

He's waiting for her to express some interest in his idea and then they both turn their heads toward the TV as they hear the words "...and once again Super Mario, Lara Croft and the Angry Birds are in town for G2G, the biggest event for gamers in the world, but this year, game-makers are trying to zap controversy..."

A young male reporter is standing outside LACC, in a segment recorded earlier in the evening, huge video game banners in the background. There's a bald-headed assassin, the Hitman; a gun-wielding Tony Soprano-type, and a near-futuristic warrior. *Satanic Realm 5* is also on display, an image of diabolical evil, serrated fangs and barbed horns, electric crimson and carmine.

"Aha," says Alejandro, smirking. "The genius of marketing."

"Online reports and social media are suggesting protests here tomorrow," says the reporter. "A leaked video from one game company, featuring homophobic comments, has upset people."

The broadcast cuts to a clip of Steve in the studio, yelling, and then to some Twitter readouts calling for a demonstration. "Other groups say minorities are being ignored by games," says the reporter. A woman in her 40s, African-American, is interviewed. "When was the last time you played a game with a hero who looked like me?" she asks.

"Dammit," says Alejandro.

"Diversity. It's the new angle for the mass media," says Kjersti. "Violence is dead."

"The timing's not good, not at all."

She doesn't want the conversation to get too far from what she came for, and what she heard him say in the bedroom, so she stays silent.

The news anchor is on screen now; she gives a look of disapproval. "It's a lot different from the days of *Space Invaders*. Remember that, Eric?"

Her co-host grins. "I remember when *Tetris* came out," he says. "If it hadn't been for the time I wasted on that game, I might be president of the network by now." Alejandro switches off the TV, looks at his cell phone and frowns.

"Now I know why so many news networks are requesting interviews," he says. "They definitely don't want to talk about *Satanic Realm 5*."

She waits as he sends some texts. "You said you had an idea," says Kjersti.

"Well, it needs some thought, some fleshing out," he says, looking up, placing his phone on the kitchen counter. "But broad brush, Saturnine. We want to launch something, an editorial platform. It'll be editorially independent, like an official magazine. You'll front it."

She stands looking at him for a moment, feels her grip tightening on her glass. He talks some more about his plan, she hears the words coming out of his mouth, a lot of dreary marketing-speak. She feels a rush of despair, a loosening of the self-control she's been struggling to maintain all day.

"You want me to shill your games? You want me to be one of your little PR minions?" She knows she's shouting.

"Kjersti. Calm down," he says, spreading his hands, a look of genuine surprise. "This could be really good for you. Let me lay it out for you."

"Don't you get it? I'm a journalist," she says. "Not a flack."

"Stop shouting," he says. "You're not making any sense."

"OK. Let me make it as clear as I can. Go fuck yourself and go fuck your dumb idea."

He walks away, shaking his head. He turns to her, and his face is angry and now he's shouting.

"Game journalism is a cesspit," he yells. "Look at this shit." He points at the TV. "Look at what you people are doing. It's completely out of control. No wonder the guys, my guys, don't want to get involved."

"I thought they wanted out because I didn't come to your little soiree."

"We need to take this back, to get a grip on this. We're spending millions of dollars and then, somehow, it all becomes about you and about morons like Steve Carter and Sheldon Tavernier and this goddamn Corruption video. That's what you needed to say tonight in your speech. Not some feeble touchy-feely crap. You fucked up, Kjersti."

"I fucked up?" She's heading for the door, enraged. "You were the one who wanted to leak that Carter thing. And now you want me to submit to your bullshit. No." And she's outside the door, and she slams it.

In the elevator, she pulls at her hair as she remembers that not only has he still not told her what she needs to know about *Satanic Realm 5*, she didn't even get to ask the question.

24

G2G 2016

9.51 a.m.

It comes back to him, the sweaty anxiety and fetishistic desire to hold the box, to take it home and be with the console and its first games.

The PlayStation 3 launch, 17 November 2006, Capital Mall, Jefferson City. He was 12 years old, so his dad must have been there too, one of the rare occasions when they went out together. He remembers looking up as his dad grimly shoved excited teenagers out of the way.

Now, almost ten years on, Charlie is being jostled in another crowd full of gamers, as they file into Los Angeles Convention Center's vast West Hall.

Harried-looking security guards check badges and search anyone unwise enough to bring a bag. There are groups of people chanting slogans and waving placards. Some are protesting homophobia, others a lack of diversity. Others have placards that say "Hands Off Our Fun." Another says, "End the Corruption." There are a few people holding joke placards that reference fictional game worlds. Guards are keeping the protestors apart.

Pretty young women in skimpy outfits hand out stuffed toys shaped like game icons: stars, coins, mushrooms—one for each person. A woman offers him a fluffy red heart. Charlie waves it away.

He is feeling nauseated with nerves, exacerbated by this unaccustomed proximity to so many other people.

He, along with a man dressed as Booker DeWitt and a woman dressed as Lara Croft, squeeze through the doors into the hall, somehow passing through the entrance as one.

In front of the great stage and its *Tetris*-style ziggety-zags of huge screens, he finds a little space to stand in. Music is playing; he recognizes it immediately—the theme from *Mario 64*.

As the crowd scuttles hurriedly to be as close as possible to the front, he holds back. He wants to be close to an emergency exit, just in case he is spotted by any of his Piranha Frenzy colleagues.

That PlayStation 3 launch day, at the mall, they had bought the machine, taken it home and played *Resistance: Fall of Man*. His father had decided the game was nothing special before embarking on a long rant against the high scores it had received in the press. Then they had played a robot combat game that his father had liked a great deal, but which Lars found clunky and dull.

Even then, his father had talked about the "criminal corruption" in game journalism. It had been his life. Now, he and his father's plan to infiltrate and expose Piranha Frenzy has come to fruition. Today, the film he has made will be shown, released onto YouTube.

It will light up a debate about game journalism that will bring its corrupt practitioners to their knees. Everything that can have been done, has been done. All Charlie can do is watch as the attack unfolds.

—⁓—

Kjersti has a VIP Access All Areas G2G badge that allows her through a small door at the side of the Convention Hall. Even from this distant place she can hear the crowds milling around, the shouting and laughing, overly loud music from various advertising tents erected among the crowds, hawking energy drinks and candy bars.

When she enters the West Hall through the side door, she can see the large numbers of people gathering in front of the stage. Normally she would be behind the stage, taking a peek out at her gathering audience, feeling the growing excitement of the moment.

Now she experiences a pang of misplacement, a knowledge of loss. Without Piranha Frenzy, she is still a recognizable face, a quasi-celebrity within the confines of video gaming's court, but she does not carry the power to draw enough people to support herself, let alone to threaten the established media giants.

She knows she is wholly replaceable. The games are the stars and it doesn't much matter if it's her or Liam or even Steve who is on the stage, whipping the crowd up to enjoy something they are already entirely prepared to enjoy to the fullest.

She heads away from the stage, threads past the various booths erected by gaming's biggest companies. They are all operational now, screens rolling through games, speakers blaring marketing mantras, while junior producers wait, controllers in hand, for the first fans of the day to come by and be impressed by their feature-rich demo-scripts.

It will be a quiet opening hour on the booths of G2G this year. So many people are at the stage, or waiting outside for the crowds to clear. In a few hours, she knows, these halls and corridors and booths will be crammed with people. Walking ten yards will take minutes, not seconds.

She makes her way toward the giant, towering Satan she had stood beneath the day before. It is looking down at the human beings below wearing an expression of absolute contempt. It is the emblem of *Satanic Realm 5*, the character she had defeated 24 hours before.

She has spent most of the night thinking of her father, wishing that she could sit with him and go through her options, rationally and carefully.

Most of the night she has struggled to find a way to commune with something of him, a memory of his good sense, his patience, his ability to analyze without the distracting color of ego and pride.

Kjersti has come away with two certainties. The first is that she needs to fight to save her career, to do the things that she wants to do, free from the machinations of the Sheldons of the world, free from the bumbling incompetence of the Brads, free from the avuncular guidance of the Franks.

The other is to clear her name, to prove that her review is right.

She has checked the message boards and forums. A few people remember *Dare You Enter the Devil's Lair?*. There is a scan of that letter from Commodore User. But mostly, she is accused of making a connection that doesn't exist. There is no word on the whereabouts of the Edwards brothers.

She arrives at the gnarled crimson feet of the devil, which double as a reception desk for Saturnine's booth. Upon enquiry, a smiling young man tells her that, unfortunately, Alejandro Bernal is in meetings all day. She can see in the man's eyes that she looks a mess, that she looks like a crazy person who hasn't slept in days.

"I'm his partner," she hears herself saying, without social varnish. "Go get him."

A minute later a velvet rope is lifted to allow her inside the booth's inner workings. A door opens and she enters. It's a meeting room, with six people, all smartly dressed, as well as Alejandro, sitting in front of a screen that's showing the Piranha Frenzy presentation.

Alejandro waves her in, invites her to take a spare seat next to him. The room is glass-walled, a gesture, she thinks, of the current corporate vogue for transparency. But also it's about Alejandro holding court, and being seen and recognized. She feels sure there are other rooms that are not open to the public gaze.

"We're just knocking around some ideas, y'know, what to do about this Corruption video thing," he says. "It's dropping on YouTube in less than an hour."

"We need to talk," she says.

Alejandro looks at her, his face full of impatience. He dismisses his staff. They file out of the room, giving her awkward smiles.

Onscreen, Sheldon walks out onto the stage to a smattering of applause.

Alejandro gestures to a chair next to him. "We'll talk," he says. "Let's watch this for a while."

On the TV, Sheldon begins a speech about the Nintendo 64, about how Nintendo has shaped gaming, how Piranha Frenzy has followed gaming since the year of its launch, and defined the way the world thinks and talks about gaming. He talks about how the past twenty years have been a joyful experience for millions of gamers.

Kjersti waits for the right moment to demand that Alejandro quits lying to her.

"We've prepared a statement," says Alejandro, answering a question that Kjersti hasn't asked. His eyes stay on the screen. "We're condemning the Scourge video as an outrageous work of biased propaganda that is entirely devoid of facts. We're distancing ourselves from Piranha Frenzy and condemning its unprofessional approach to the world's biggest entertainment business."

Onscreen, the camera pans across the crowd. It's immense, thousands of people waving stars and mushrooms, cheering and shouting. This is the largest crowd she has ever seen at G2G. There are some banners too, placards with slogans.

"I'm sorry, about last night," he says, still watching the screen.

One of gaming's most feted developers is introduced onscreen, and he strides onto the stage. A wave of applause and cheers rises from the crowd as the man, well into his 60s, bobs his head and waves, a large smile on his face. He is beloved.

In stilted English, the Japanese man reads out a short, bland statement about the power of games to unite humanity and is greeted with rapturous applause. But as soon as he is done, chants come from the crowd, rival chants that Kjersti cannot understand.

Liam Sullivan arrives on stage and runs through a little quiz game with the crowd, questions about Nintendo 64 launch game *Mario 64*. It was a section originally intended for Kjersti.

"He's very good," says Alejandro. "But he's not as good as you."

"He is better than I am," she says.

Images appear on the giant screens around the stage, and Liam belts out a question.

"Where does this guy live?" A concretish square with red eyes and wonky teeth is onscreen.

The answer is roared back, a collective pool of knowledge.

'Whomp's Fortress!'"

But still, the chanting, the shouting, an ugly sound. The event producer, Kjersti notices, has stopped broadcasting images of the crowd.

She looks at Alejandro. They have been together for a few months. It's been an intense affair. She has enjoyed him, enjoyed the trappings of his life, the tasteful downtown apartment, the expense account. She has enjoyed his wit and humor, his insight.

"What does the little fella carry when he follows Mario about?" Liam is shouting, showing a new character.

"A camera," says Alejandro, a second before the crowd roars its answer back. He smiles.

She has come here to tell him that they are finished. Yet there is also this about him; the things that attracted her in the first place, his charm and his ability to move through the world unimpeded and unafraid.

"What's this Koopa Troopa's name?"

"Koopa the Quick," says Kjersti, flatly.

He smiles at her.

Onstage, Liam looks happy, performing his role magnificently. He says his goodbyes and a roar of "more" goes up. It's obvious that Liam has connected with them. But this crowd, she thinks, would stand there all day long answering trivia questions about games.

The chanting, which had seemed to subside during the quiz, begins again. She catches words here and there. "Corruption," "Lies," "Hate."

Alejandro turns to her, takes her hands. "Let's get away from all this, tonight," he says. "Let's talk it out. We deserve to give each other that. Let's not do this here." She smiles, but slips her hands free.

Steve Carter trots on stage wearing a Piranha Frenzy T-shirt, receives cheers from patches of fans in the crowd. He says that a short film has been prepared, and reads something from a teleprompter.

There's a shot of Brad and Sheldon standing together at the corner of the stage, looking up at the immense screens, waiting for the film to begin. They look worried.

"You lied to me," she says to Alejandro. "I want the truth. Not tonight. Now."

Steve pauses midway through his routine. Someone in the crowd is shouting at him. There is confusion on his face. She catches a chant coming up from the audience. "Hater."

There's a new chant also, from another section of the crowd. "Steve, Steve, Steve."

"This is getting out of hand," says Alejandro, a frown on his face.

"Look at me, Alex," she says. "Answer me."

"Not now," he says. "After this. I promise."

Steve is looking at the crowd and looking at the camera. His facial expression passes from triumph to fear and back again. He brings the mic up toward his face, opens his mouth.

—⚬—

The very second that Steve raises his mic to speak to the crowd, the realization of defeat slams into Sheldon.

He can see, as surely any sensible person can, that Steve needs to get off the stage, and let their nice promotional film take over.

But Steve is not sensible, and Sheldon knows for sure that whatever words fall from his mouth will make the situation worse.

Sheldon understands, as Steve smirks and opens his mouth, addressing directly the small group of protesters, that his own assumption that all would work out fine was vanity and foolishness, and this understanding, this clarity, also brings into focus the events of the night before, the burglary that had allowed him to go home, secure in the mistaken knowledge that he would prevail.

The words that come out of Steve's mouth are, "I want to thank my fans for all the support you've shown me over the past 24 hours. As you know, a private video of me was released that seemed to suggest I have a problem with Liam being gay and with gays in general."

Sheldon arrives at a deep comprehension of this unfolding reality. It isn't Steve's stupidity that is killing me, he thinks, it is my own.

And yet, while the Steve crisis plays out, Sheldon cannot quite address the details of this reality, cannot grasp some fundamental and urgent reality. His mind cannot escape the spectacle of Steve suiciding his own career.

Steve is saying that he has no problem with blacks or women or anyone else who is "different." He is making some point about people always complaining, always trying to spoil the fun.

Steve says he was a mere shop assistant ten years ago, and now he's a successful media personality. Anyone can do it.

Sheldon knows what Steve is going to say next. "Instead of complaining and whining about things that don't matter, let's just have some fun! Video games. Yeah!"

Steve strides across the stage, triumphant, hands the mic to Sheldon, and makes some grand swirling hand gesture designed to tell someone, somewhere to run the video.

He walks past Sheldon and tries the door to backstage, but it's locked, so he heads to some steps by the side of the stage. As he passes again, Sheldon grabs his arm. Steve smiles, anticipating praise.

"Hey, superstar," snarls Sheldon. "You're fired."

—w—

The video begins, a short piece of propaganda for Piranha Frenzy. People around Charlie begin to cheer, but Steve's appearance on stage seems to have made the general bad feeling worse. The event has descended from a celebration to something edgier and ugly.

"Fucking dickhead," yells a man beside him. Others are disagreeing, and the atmosphere takes on a nasty note.

For Charlie, this is an unwelcome diversion. His moment has arrived. Much hard work has been poured into the events of the next few moments.

It was decided, some weeks ago, to hack the computers that are currently running the Piranha Frenzy film, and replace it with the final documentary, The ROTTEN CORRUPTION at the Heart of Video Game Reviews.

This had proven to be a challenging problem for the Robys. It was decided that hired men needed to be brought in to take care of this tricky, technical task. Fortunately, Charlie's dad knows a number of associates who said they could handle a job like this.

Equally problematic has been deciding when to run the documentary. Charlie and his dad argued for weeks about whether to jump in at the beginning of Piranha Frenzy's puff-piece, halfway through, or near the end.

It was agreed, in the end, that depriving the fans of their slice of nostalgia would probably do more harm than good, and, in any case, set next to the sort of self-promoting nonsense Piranha Frenzy's short was likely to portray, the critical documentary might even exercise a little more emotive power.

It was decided to pretend, publicly, that the documentary would be released an hour after Piranha Frenzy's presentation, just to avoid any unwelcome last-minute checks and defenses by the LACC audiovisual team. But instead, they had agreed to show it from the stage, and release it on YouTube at the same time.

And so the official Piranha Frenzy commercial runs, loud music, classic game footage, a few interview snippets from games execs, former Piranha Frenzy people being goofy, some vintage footage of the early days of the company. It's a clear attempt to bind the website to the events its reporters have been covering all these years as if, thinks Charlie, the media ought to be congratulated for the success of video games.

The crowd seems slightly mollified, there's cheering as the film builds toward a climactic end, and... the screen goes blank. A great groan goes up at what seems to be some technical error.

Charlie knows this is the moment. The hackers have done their work. Words appear.

"The documentary you are about to see is now available on YouTube. Search 'Scourge of Corruption.'"

This fades to "The ROTTEN CORRUPTION at the Heart of Video Game Reviews." The screen goes black. "A film by Lars Roby, aka Charlie Black, formerly Piranha Frenzy news editor, undercover investigator."

The crowd understands what's happening. They know about the blog post. Alongside Kjersti Wong's review and Steve Carter's rant, it's been dominating gaming's news sites for 12 hours, has even been trending on Twitter.

Cheering and jeering rise from the gathering, a swell of appreciation at this unexpected Easter egg. Charlie sees Sheldon looking up at the screen. Brad is trying to open a stage door to get to the video room. It's locked. Charlie reckons they'll see about thirty seconds of the film before someone, literally, begins pulling out plugs.

—⁓—

Kjersti sits quietly through the Piranha Frenzy reel. She's seen it before. Alejandro spends the first minute calling Steve Carter various unpleasant names and asking why the hell he hasn't been fired.

"How can we have people like this representing us?" he demands, as if Piranha Frenzy's employees were somehow answerable to him. She has seen this before in him, the sense of ownership over game media.

Then he moves onto the amateurish nature of the reel, forgetting Kjersti's part in its creation, saying that it "looks like something from 2012." This is where he is at his most animated, she thinks, in the evaluation of advertising reels.

The office door opens and the young man from reception walks in. He smiles at Kjersti now. He's carrying a small brown envelope; he places it in front of Alejandro and says, "As requested, directly to you."

Alejandro's hand goes to the package, but Kjersti grabs his forearm. The brown envelope is slightly too small for its contents, a single oblong. It might be an iPhone or a deck of cards.

"It's a cassette, isn't it?" she says.

He stands up and she rises with him, he shakes her loose, grabs the package. She stumbles to the ground. She looks up at him, shocked. His mouth is open, he is panicking. One hand goes to his cheek. Then he turns away and puts the package in his inside jacket pocket.

Behind his head, she sees the screen go blank.

By the time Lars Roby's film has begun, the room is filling up with a rush of marketing people, who don't know whether to look at the screen, or to look at Kjersti Wong, sprawled on the floor. Alejandro stands over her, desperately pulling her up.

—⁓—

Sheldon looks up and sees Charlie on the screen, sitting in his private office, in his own chair.

His mind registers the thing he was trying to locate while Steve was making his idiot speech. That the computer and the cell phone and the film he had snatched last night, was all fakery, a dummy. That a guy who bugs his own bosses and dresses up as a robot in order to eavesdrop at a company party is absolutely guaranteed to leave a booby trap at his house.

"Hello, my name is Lars Roby. I am working undercover at Piranha Frenzy as news editor Charlie Black. My mission is to make a documentary that demonstrates the corruption and dirty-dealing that goes on at a large game website."

So, Charlie had created an extra film, a bad film that offered no damaging revelations. He had left his house vulnerable. He had even organized a house party so that his home address would be known and the geography of his house remembered. And all so that Sheldon would go to his house and view a fake film and retire to bed the night before G2G and not be worried enough about the release of a hostile documentary to figure out that it would be hacked through the company's own screening of its marketing reel.

Charlie's film cuts to the Big Meeting Room. Sheldon sees himself, Brad Hoffman and Alejandro Bernal. The picture isn't perfect, the audio is muffled. A caption appears underneath the three men in the room.

"Secretly taped meeting between game publisher Saturnine and senior editorial execs at Piranha Frenzy's offices - May 2016." Bubbles pop up above the men, indicating their names and job titles.

Sheldon sees that Brad is still struggling with the stage door, is banging on the door, looking around for a security person. Sheldon remembers that the film is already on

YouTube. He takes out his cell, goes to The Scourge's page and waits for the film to load. He doesn't want to miss it.

The audio focuses in. The picture clears.

Onscreen, Alejandro Bernal is speaking. "Obviously we've had a long relationship and at difficult times like these, it's good to know who your friends are. We're fully committed to backing *Satanic Realm 5* because we believe, truly, that it's going to get a lot of positive press and a hatful of glowing reviews."

Sheldon says, "We certainly hope so."

There's an ooohing and aaahing in the crowd. Sheldon looks out at them. He sees some pushing and shoving. People still arguing about the Steve Carter thing, but the chanting has ceased. The crowd is entranced, some glare at him.

He thinks, "I didn't take a bribe."

Alejandro Bernal: "Ah, 'hope.' There's a word we don't use much at Saturnine. We're more interested in certainties. As I'm sure you are. The certainty of knowing, for example, that you'll hit your ad targets this quarter. I mean, our marketing budget for this game is huge, and we want to make sure we spend it wisely."

Brad: "Well, obviously we have a church and state policy here, and..."

Sheldon: "What Brad means is that we can make no guarantees, but look, we know the pedigree of this series, we know what you guys can do. Just take a look at our review of the last game."

Sheldon didn't take a bribe. But he knows what he said and he knows what he meant and he knows that there will be no hiding.

A security guard has been spotted by Brad, making his way slowly through the crowd, a large bunch of keys on his hip. Soon the video will be stopped. Sheldon knows trying to stop this from playing out is going to be a bad mistake.

—⁂—

Kjersti stands up. Alejandro tries to apologize, but she brushes him away. Alejandro is speaking onscreen. It's as if everyone in the meeting room is holding their breath. They are all looking at the screen.

Alejandro: "Obviously I am not here to strong-arm you guys into giving me a perfect score. I am just looking for an assurance that we understand each other here."

Sheldon: "We do, Alejandro. We absolutely do."

Alejandro: "Because this is a fat lot of cash we're looking to spend with you, on one game, and a lot of my colleagues have been saying for a long time that money spent with the specialist press is money wasted."

Sheldon: "Which is a discussion I am always happy to engage in. If you look at the stats..."

Alejandro: "Sure Shel, sure. But ultimately, the only stat we are interested in is the review score."

Brad: "I don't think you need to have any concerns on that score [laughs nervously]. We're never going to make any guarantees about review scores; that would be unethical, but I think we can safely say that you're going to be well looked after."

Sheldon: "Well looked after, Alejandro, no nasty surprises. As always, we are at your service."

The film cuts to Charlie in an empty Piranha Frenzy newsroom. He is introducing a sequence about the fake news stories he has dropped onto the site.

"Get me a new draft of our reaction," says Alejandro. His marketing people are already moving around. "Make sure it's extremely critical of Lars Roby and of all these bastards. Make sure it says I was taken out of context. Set up some media interviews. We're getting in front of this. It's about them. Not us."

Charlie is onscreen, talking about lax editorial standards, a culture of chasing traffic before all else. Kjersti is staring at Alejandro, waiting for them all to leave.

"They made me look like a sleazebag," he says to her.

"Relax," she says. "At least they don't know about you pushing your girlfriend over."

"I... I'm sorry. It was an accident. I just can't afford to..."

There's some footage onscreen of people yelling at each other, in a meeting that Kjersti knows nothing about. She sees the CEO and the advertising manager.

"This is what you always wanted isn't it, Alejandro," she says, gesturing toward the screen. "The humbling of the press. Now the critics are destroyed, you are free of them."

He eyes her, warily.

"You know they'll try to make you look like the bad guy," she says. "Just as you are trying to lay it all on them."

"I didn't mean to hurt you. It's just..."

And then the screen dies.

An image comes up, of the crowd. They are silent. No one is moving. Alejandro and Kjersti stand, watch, and wait for the reaction.

—⁂—

Straight after the Alejandro Bernal meeting scene, Charlie starts to make his way to the emergency exit. The security guard stationed there is on a walkie-talkie. Charlie waits, lurks as the film goes on.

He's managed way more airtime than he'd expected. He can see that members of the audience are anticipating that the film will be shut off and are searching on their phones.

The film stops. After a few seconds silence, booing rises from the crowd, angry shouts. People begin clustering to watch videos on mobiles that are successfully streaming.

A security guard steps onto the stage and says that, for security reasons, the hall is going to be closed for an hour, and can everyone leave the building quietly please.

A few people turn toward the exits but most are stock-still and visibly angry. They can see no reason to leave.

The booing intensifies. There's shouting, cursing. They are asking for the film to be put back on. Curse words are yelled. Some begin to throw things, their stars and hearts and fluffy items. There is shoving and shouting and yells of "calm down."

Charlie heads for the exit. He can see people pushing one another, some trying to get out, others picking up the items, seeming, perhaps, to take advantage of the chaos and collect a full set of fluffy toys.

He looks back at the stage. A man dressed as Bowser has climbed up and has the mic, roaring obscenities. Some others join him. The security guard intervenes but is pushed back. He retreats. The fans begin pulling at cutouts on the stage wall, the images of game characters.

Charlie spots Sheldon being helped off the stage by a group of fans, and then he disappears into the crowd.

Security guards are making urgent entreaties on their walkie-talkies, someone begins blowing a whistle, people start screaming. Charlie is scared now.

He sees a Kratos being knocked over and fighting, real fighting between two small groups of men. The security guard has opened the emergency exit, and many people are pushing, and he pushes too and as soon as he is outside he sprints into the sunlight, breathing so deeply that he's panting uncontrollably and thinking three frightening words over and over again.

I did this.

—ᴍ—

The nice people who helped him down from the stage are gone and Sheldon realizes he is in a stew of very scared people, pushing away from the stage, trying to get toward the exits. There is a strong smell of sweat, of fear.

He can see the aisles that stream past the giant game booths are already packed and stoppered with people, and that they have spilled onto the floor of the booths themselves. Any sense of orderly progress is diminishing. He feels something exploding within himself, panic.

There are people, elbowing others aside, gathering up the fluffy toys, and yelling. The crowd squeezes together and, collectively, gasps for air. Sheldon crouches and buries his face into the back of a woman and waits.

He feels a sense of surprise at how real this all is, how absolutely not like it's happening elsewhere to someone else, and this connection brings him to the conclusion of the thought-train that began when Steve raised that mic to his lips.

He cannot cease to think of his predicament in terms of a game design flaw. It's like a real-time strategy game. You begin, weak and vulnerable, with hardly any resources, and your only concern is survival.

In midgame, if you are still alive, you seek to make smart moves and use your resources carefully. If you are smart you time your attacks perfectly, in order to progress as quickly as possible.

It is the late game that Sheldon has been living, for so long now. The part of the game where your enemies are humbled, your armies and your buildings are so powerful that there is really very little to do except clear up any remnants of resistance and amuse yourself in any small and cruel way that you can.

Sheldon has always been extremely good at playing this game. In fact, he's been the best. The game is Sheldon's life, getting away from Petersham, Massachusetts and grabbing a job writing about games and then climbing through promotions and job titles and then gathering his power toward himself and taking it away from those around him.

He has been so good at this game, he did not notice when it ceased to be a game—when it became as serious as real life.

Crouching here, sobbing onto the back of this woman, hoping not to be crushed to death, he cannot view anything that is happening in a way that is remotely ironic or removed.

The woman twirls away from him and he stumbles into a group of people, waiting to get out, protecting one another. A man recognizes him, "This is your fault, you idiot," the man yells.

His girlfriend or wife shoves at him and more names are called. He falls away from them and as he loses his footing he looks up at a very large man in cosplay, dressed as Ganon, and holding his warrior's sword high above the crowd to preserve it from damage, and as Sheldon tumbles toward him the man turns away and Sheldon's feet are no longer beneath him and his jaw meets Ganon's elbow in a crunch that everyone within ten feet hears very well, but which Sheldon does not hear at all.

— ∿ —

People are pressed against the glass wall of the office, crowded and squeezed and scared. The corridors are jammed with people. Alejandro looks ashen.

"It's mayhem," he says, unnecessarily. "This is dangerous."

"We should go," says Kjersti.

"No," he says. "It's safer here."

There's no sign of the marketing people. Kjersti guesses they are no longer fretting about press statements.

One of the people pressed against the glass wall recognizes Alejandro and soon there are faces glaring at them and shouting. The noise in the hall is unlike anything she has heard before.

A serious woman wearing, incongruously, an Atari T-shirt, opens the door to the meeting room and says, "Out, now."

Even if Kjersti and Alejandro had been tempted to ignore her, a voice comes over the LACC intercom telling everyone to remain calm and make their way to the exits, before saying the words, "This is an emergency."

The woman moves into the room and yells again. "Out!" and two men are with her and they are prizing the TV screen off the wall. It blinks off.

Alejandro gazes at them for a moment. Kjersti pushes him toward the door. The glass wall begins to collapse behind them. It falls to the ground in one piece and the people on the other side are in the office, standing on the wall, seeking out space and escape.

Kjersti grabs hold of Alejandro's hand and they make their way onto the booth's main area, which is a scene of chaos. Groups of people are pulling apart the exhibits and ripping out the consoles, PCs and TV screens that are showing the games. Image cutouts of game logos and game characters are under the arms of people, who have ripped them from the walls.

They begin trotting toward the exits. The floors are packed with people, most of them frightened, a few engaged in looting, carrying their booty under their arms or in groups.

Standing beneath the giant Satan, Alejandro is frantically looking for a way out, something that does not involve joining the common herd as it streams, painfully slowly, toward the distant exits.

The glass-wall people are behind them now. "Bernal, you fucking lowlife," shouts one of them. They are grabbing him, punching him and pulling him down. Frantically, he twists to free himself. His jacket is ripped and comes loose.

Kjersti pulls him into the crowd, away from his assailants. She sees the brown envelope fall from his ripped jacket, onto the floor. It disappears under the feet of the crowd. She freezes for a moment, but there is no way back, no way to collect the cassette from under the feet of hundreds of frightened people.

Alejandro's head is down and they are moving through the crowd, away from the angry people. Now the shouting has become the sound of crying and people comforting one another, children held high above the madness.

Alejandro holds Kjersti's hand, very tightly. They fold themselves into the crowd, allow themselves to go along, acceptingly, toward the exit.

25

DOOM

1:25 p.m.

In the tranquility of his office, Sheldon is dabbing a wet tissue against his busted lip, using an iPad as a mirror.

Not entirely satisfied with his nursing skills, he gives up the effort, puts down his iPad and turns on the large TV screen, flicks to a 24-hour news channel.

A ticker reads, "Riot at Video Game Convention; Minor Injuries Reported." Images show footage of enraged people, some dressed as video game characters, running amok in the convention hall, ripping down signs, grabbing marketing artifacts and electronic equipment, tearing apart the console modules displaying new games.

Others are trying to stop them, or are making for the exits, panicked. It is an ugly scene.

The news cuts to a reporter interviewing another journalist. They stand in front of the Piranha Frenzy stage, stuff strewn about the floor, clothing, the head of a Donkey Kong Jr. A few cops are standing about in the background in front of the company logo. A scrolling caption reads "Police Say Convention Center Now Quiet." The riot is over.

"We've heard that gaming is violent, but this is like something out of Doom," says one of the reporters.

The other reporter says, "The gamers came for freebies and tchotchkes, and left with TVs and games consoles. They've stripped the convention hall clean."

Underneath the reporters, a new caption scrolls across the screen, "G2G 2016

Games Convention Cancelled Following Gamer Riot."

After being knocked out by Ganon, Sheldon had recalled nothing until regaining consciousness on a stretcher, near a medical vehicle in the bright sunshine of a parking lot. Other people with injuries were being tended to, including some distressed children.

He checked his phone. It was gone.

He wandered off. No one stopped him. Further from the Convention Center, it was clear that there would be no cabs. Police vehicles were parked in zigs and zags all over streets closed to other vehicles. Sheldon staggered about, still dazed, in the general direction of the offices, noticed for the first time wetness on his shirt, on his face, tasted the blood in his mouth.

He rounded a corner and saw men and women being herded into police trucks, loot scattered about the floor. These were the ones who had been too slow getting away from the scene before the police arrived.

Marketing signs piled up, even some human-sized statues, TV screens, office furniture, boxes of soda cans. The media cameras were there too, and this had alarmed Sheldon enough to keep his head down, and so he eventually found his way to the normality of Los Angeles' downtown streets and from there to his place of work, to the sanctity of his office.

The offices of Piranha Frenzy are deserted.

On TV, a politician is on the line, talking to the anchor, babbling about violence in video games. He says that the "chickens have come home to roost."

They cut to an image of a crying woman, wearing an Elizabeth outfit, her clothing all wonky, her make-up awry. But the politician interview audio runs over her image. The young woman's testimony has already run a dozen times. They've moved on.

Nodding, the anchor addresses camera. "We're hearing that the riot was sparked by the showing of a short fan-made film, something that obviously made the crowd very angry. We'll get more on that film later."

Sheldon groans, switches the TV off.

Hearing a noise outside his office, a disturbance in the air-conditioned equilibrium, Sheldon looks up. Through the glass door of his office, he sees, standing almost frozen, Charlie Black. Ridiculously, Charlie is in tip-toe Scooby-Doo mode.

"Really, Charlie? Not enough drama for one day?"

"It's Lars." Charlie straightens himself.

Sheldon ignores the correction. "Why are you here, Charlie? More sneaky footage?"

"I'm just picking up my cameras. I didn't want to disturb you."

"You didn't want to disturb me?" Sheldon is laughing now. "Are you kidding me?"

Charlie steps into the office, gestures toward a chair.

"Oh sure," says Sheldon. "Make yourself comfortable. Maybe I can fix you a cocktail?"

Charlie sits. "Er...no...that's fine. I don't drink."

There's a moment's silence.

"So Charlie, is your old man happy now, does he feel like his vengeance has been sated?"

"I haven't spoken to him yet."

"I guess he got me good. I mean, he's dedicated the last fifteen years to trying to screw me, so it'll probably feel great. For him. For a few days anyhow."

Sheldon's mind races toward the ramifications of the day, the endless inquiries, media interviews, blame and denial.

"Of course, poor old dad, his son's career is completely over, because, well, hiring someone who makes undercover films about his employer is generally a red flag for HR. That must make you sad, Charlie. You had promise..."

"It's Lars. I'll have a career..."

"You'll have a career stroking the excited genitalia of your fellow inmates at whatever penitentiary they throw you in, because, mark my words Charlie, you and your old man are going to jail for this."

Sheldon surprises himself. Facing the catastrophe of his career imploding, his power slipping away, his reputation in ruins, Charlie's appearance has given him a shot of energy.

"I don't think so," says Charlie. "We showed a film. We can't be held responsible."

"You hacked into a public performance and as a direct result a riot ensued, costing millions of dollars, harming the reputation of an entire multi-billion dollar industry, and causing who knows how many injuries. At the very least, pal, you're going to court. It's not like Los Angeles is short of entertainment industry lawyers, spoiling for a fight."

"That'll be just another opportunity to highlight what you have been doing here. Your crimes."

Sheldon sighs. "There are no crimes, Charlie. Just some run-of-the-mill corporate bullshit."

"Crimes," says Charlie again his voice becoming louder, shriller. "You are a criminal."

"It seems an odd thing to dedicate your life to, corruption in video game journalism," says Sheldon. "I mean, the banks are still screwing everyone. The politicians, the NRA, the NSA, the KKK. There are lots of bad people in the world to investigate who've done a lot worse than crooked game reviewers."

Charlie stands up. "This will be the end of you, Sheldon. I'm not sorry. You're a bad influence on gaming. You've taken journalism and turned it into a craven whore." He's quoting his father, thinks Sheldon, who instantly recalls the strange phrase from its repeated use in A Broken Promise.

Sheldon wonders how this conversation will be reported back to the bitter oracle himself, the old man, and then has a horrible thought.

"You're not recording this are you, Charlie? No secret camera or mics. Because really..."

"No. We're done. No more recordings. I guarantee."

"Oh well, since you give me your word, clearly you're a fellow to be trusted."

"I'm going now."

Despite his injuries, Sheldon feels the need to fight. Frightened, cowering by the stage, he had wanted to run and hide. Now, he feels a sense of clarity, a belief that he is exactly where he belongs.

He realizes he actually wants to get out in front of the press, to tear into his puppet CEO, to tell the advertising manager to go fuck herself, to absolutely, utterly lay waste to Alejandro Bernal and Saturnine, to crush, mercilessly, anyone who gets in his way.

"Tell your dad this," he says. "Tell your dad that I can't wait to eat him alive in court. Tell him I'm not going down. I'll survive this. I'll dedicate the rest of my life to the same thing I've dedicated all my life to, Sheldon Tavernier. I guess me and him have got that in common, right?"

Charlie blinks. Says nothing.

Sheldon knows it's partly bluff. Without staging a coup d'état, without the help of a bright thing like Kjersti Wong, he'll be out on the street before the end of the day. But he has to start the fight back someplace.

"Now get the fuck out of here, Charlie. And no, you can't go and retrieve your bugs and planted gadgets. The lawyers are going to want to see them. I'll just have security escort you out."

Sheldon starts making calls. He wonders if any of Piranha Frenzy's video equipment has survived the riot. He needs the video guys back from G2G. He's going to make a statement. Record it, send it to the press, give them something else to play on their 24-hour channels.

He is fighting to survive. He feels the cold world of "media consultancy" beckoning, the witheringly polite acceptance of his business cards at conventions, the sucking up to people who he regards as pond life.

No, he won't let that happen to him. He thinks of himself gathering the remnants of his beleaguered forces for a *StarCraft 2* counterattack, and then rejects the comparison.

"It's not a game," he says. And he starts writing emails.

26

CONTROL

3:14 p.m.

By the sherbet rainbow arcade machines, she stands and waits for Sheldon; gazes as the attention-starved machines scroll endlessly through the motions of their rolling presets, hieroglyphic tableaux of destruction.

She'd emailed Sheldon back, stating when and where she wanted the meeting to take place. He would, she felt sure, appreciate her not being dumb enough to just show up in the padded lair of his personal office.

Ignoring *Gauntlet, Galaga* and *Punch-Out*, she approaches the coffee machine, presses buttons for a decaf without milk, sips, waits in the office-hum semi-silence.

Once she and Alejandro had escaped from the Convention Center, they had walked, silently and urgently, through the crowds of media and curious onlookers, deep into the part of town graced by the best downtown hotels. They found a hotel restaurant. He sat, disheveled, silently staring into space. Then he apologized, again and again. She couldn't tell if he was sorry for pushing her over, or for the brown envelope. Not knowing what else to do, seeking to gather herself, she ordered lunch for them both.

Snatches of conversations in the dining room wafted past, words about how the gamers had gone nuts, wild rumors of a conflagration of geek madness.

As soon as the waiter left with their order, Alejandro seemed to come to his senses. He looked long at her and said, "Have you got a phone?"

She gave her phone to him. He swiped the screen, pressed an app, placed it down in front of them. It was the voice recorder, switched on.

"Ask me," he said.

She looked at him. "OK," she said. "Tell me."

He paused for a moment, took a long draft of water.

"They came to me a year ago, the board," he said. "They wanted something big placed into this summer's schedule. They insisted on a Satanic Realm game. I told them it could not be done so quickly. It was idiotic. The next game was three years off.

"They said, 'Just do it, Alejandro. We have to make our quarterly targets.' The development people, they said it outright, they'd have to make some shortcuts. They scrambled to pull together designs and puzzles that didn't need too much thinking about. They plundered the archives. They were encouraged to just get it done.

"They actually sat in an offsite and reminisced about games and puzzles, and tried to rework them in a Satanic Realm setting. If someone wanted to deviate too much, they were told, 'Let's just stay with what works.'

"Back at the office, one of the designers started talking about some old shareware he'd played as a kid. He was one of those washed-up bearded types, always living in the past. Anyway, he brought it in, rigged up an old Commodore 64. We played it. Everyone loved the purity of the thing, how unusual it seemed, like a lost artifact from some alien culture.

"The puzzles were documented and updated and soon they were part of the design document and then the backstory and the characters and the jokes were in the game."

"*Dare You Enter the Devil's Lair?*" she says. "Why?"

"Pressure. Coming up with new stuff takes ages. The approval process costs money. The higher-ups saw this stuff and waved it through."

"You didn't warn them that you might get caught?"

"I said, 'Let's market this as a tribute to the classics,' but when we focus-tested that approach, it bombed. Gamers are sick of being sold old stuff dressed up as new, so we decided to sell them rehashed stuff, and just not mention that we'd been plundering this old game. The goddamn bean-counters insisted. And I had to sell it. I had to sell this half-assed game. It's my job."

"Why didn't you tell me this before?"

"Because we have to have some walls between us, Kjersti. You're a journalist. I'm a marketer. But here's the big joke. My bosses believe that I really did tell you this stuff, and that you put it in the review to scoop the universe."

"Will you be fired?"

He shakes his head. "I might have survived. I might have gone in hard, threatened to take them all down with me, but now..." he nodded at the iPhone. "This is my confession. I owe you that."

He had reached across the table and held her hand. She could not tell if he was relieved or depressed. "I'm sorry," he said. "About everything." She nodded and left.

Now, in the office, Sheldon arrives.

"Ah. Coffee," he says, as if it were an answer to all his ills, a resolution to the impending obliteration of his career, the humiliation of Charlie's show, his central role in a video game convention riot. She's surprised at how animated he seems.

As he makes his way to the machine, begins pressing buttons, she wonders what the hell he wants. His email has just said, "Come. It will be worth your time."

He places his coffee on the one flat surface that the top of an *Afterburner* cabinet can offer, rubs his hands, and says, "OK, Kjersti, let's talk."

"Do you think he might have bugged the coffee machine?" she asks, conspiratorially, semi-serious.

He laughs. "Charlie's bugging days are done. I think we're safe now."

She notices his cut lip, points toward it. "A war wound?"

"It's no less than I deserve," he says. "Charlie's movie, the Steve Carter thing, your review, the riot, they're hard lessons. They've allowed me to understand that we have an image problem."

She scoffs. "Really, Sheldon. Image? That's your hard lesson?"

"Hear me out," he says, frowning. "The reason for this trouble is that we have been behaving badly. You can call it lazy or corrupt or compromised but, yeah, we have to change. I have to change."

He pauses, as if waiting for her permission to continue. She gives him nothing. She does not want to be pulled into his performance.

"I guess I needed this lesson to make myself understand that the world has moved on, that the old certainties are dead."

"Isn't it late in the day to be talking of lessons?"

He looks at her, an ember of outrage in his eyes, in the dying light of his power over her.

"Yes," he says, "I am fucked."

"What do you want from me?"

He sips his coffee. Takes his time to place it back on the arcade cabinet.

"Any time now, our glorious CEO is going to come through the door. The first thing he's going to do is fire my ass. If I want to avoid that happening, I have to take preventative measures, very rapid, very bold preventative measures."

She thinks of him as an old-fashioned cartoon, sitting in a basket under a giant balloon deflating over a scorched landscape of spear-wielding cannibals, desperately unburdening his basket of anything nonessential.

"So, what's the plan?" she asks.

He looks surprised. "I want you to be the new editor-in-chief, of course."

Kjersti laughs. "Of course, Sheldon. Why didn't I just guess?" She bunches her hair at the back of her head. "You called me a nasty name and tried to deny it, you killed my review, you fired my friend. But, hey, Kjersti, come and be my EIC."

He shrugs. "Everything you've said is true and I ought to be punished. So punish me. Say no and I'll sit here and wait for the CEO and he'll hire a new EIC who'll be a place-filler, just like Brad. Just say 'no' and I'll be finished. And you can go off and launch your thing and we can all live in joyous obscurity."

"What about Brad?"

"Brad's done, whatever happens. I can't save him even if I wanted to, which I don't. Brad was another one of my mistakes. He's a reason why we're here."

"You're blaming him?"

"No. You misunderstand. I hired him because I thought I had all the answers and I needed a lackey to do what I wanted. But I was wrong. I had it all wrong. I need someone strong, not someone weak."

"How does hiring me save you?"

"We do the deal. I'll stand in front of a camera, apologizing, groveling, whatever. I'll speak about a senior management culture that was hostile to editorial integrity. Then I introduce you as the new EIC, outline the fresh, new editorial direction."

"What about the fact that I wrote a review yesterday which you claimed was libelous and untrue."

"I'll back you. I'll say it's come to my attention that..."

"Just shut up, Sheldon. For once in your life stop believing that lies can get you out of trouble."

He stares at her.

"Alejandro told me the truth," she says. "They copied a ton of stuff in *Dare You Enter the Devil's Lair?*. He wants me to break the story, maybe in a few days, after all this has died down."

"Alejandro told you that? Why did he do that?"

"If you have to ask that question, Sheldon, you'll never understand the answer."

He smiles. "That's fair. So let me worry about the stuff I do understand, which is that we need each other, right now, and today is the day we come out fighting, the day we break Alejandro's confession."

"This doesn't stop the CEO from firing you, and then me."

"Let me worry about that."

"No, Sheldon. I don't want half the story."

"OK." he says. His hands arrange the invisible pieces in front of him, like giant Lego bricks. "If I'm in control, if I'm making the moves, the focus of the shareholders moves to the CEO and to the suits. I'll be taking charge, moving the narrative forward, while the suits are fiddling. The shareholders will want someone's head. Better the CEO than me. Obviously, I'll have to make some calls. Well, in truth, I've been making calls and sending emails for a few hours now."

"A coup d'état, a revolution, with me as your Marianne, your emblem?"

"With you as my partner."

She laughs without humor. "Are you delusional? Do you think they are going to give you the CEO's job? You were the one on the video. You're the one who was caught with his pants down."

"That's all horseshit," he says, anger rising in his voice. "Charlie Black is a fool. You take that film apart, and there's nothing there. I didn't promise Saturnine a damned thing. I said they'd be looked after. That's all. It's the kind of nonsense that gets said in meetings. It's just smoothing the way, being agreeable. You think the shareholders don't get that? They spend their lives bullshitting to people in meetings. It's just business."

"Alejandro believed you would be too chicken-shit to run a negative score. And he was right. It's corruption. You're corrupt."

"The game looks like an 85 percenter," he says. "We all just expected things to fall into place. Out of the hundred or so reviews out there, yours was the only one that didn't score it above 75."

"I screwed up, by being honest?"

"No ... you did your job. You did good. I did not. Charlie caught me looking like a sleazeball because that's how I've been behaving. It's time to change."

She considers her future of sitting in meetings with this man and listening to what he says and doing what he wants, and the certainty comes to her that she won't do that. She'd rather go back to Norway and play MMOs.

"No," she says. "I'm not interested."

But she knows she cannot ignore that she is being offered the job as EIC of the world's biggest game website. The thought of how much she wants this is fearsome to her.

She can feel ambition bloom within her, she can feel the attraction of the offer. She'll be feted by the mainstream, make appearances on the big networks. She can interview whoever she likes, whenever she likes. She can write what she likes and she can address an immense audience.

Then there's the pay increase, an escape from her house-share. There's heading up the planning meetings, deciding what gets published, what doesn't, promoting the good people, getting rid of the talentless and the sycophants. There's re-inventing game journalism from the top-down, not from the bottom-up. She knows she cannot ignore this opportunity.

She looks at Sheldon, looks at him so hard she is almost looking into him. Gone is the smirking, all-powerful office-tyrant. He is a desperate man.

"You are going to hear my offer," she says.

He looks surprised. Nods.

"You are going to make me EIC," she says. "You will place no one above me. Ever. You will guarantee to operate a completely hands-off approach to all editorial operations. No meddling. You don't even get to come to the meetings. You will guarantee my position for a minimum of five years. You will freeze all editorial costs, no cuts without my permission. All hiring and firing is my domain entirely. I get video, design, engineering, overseas, social, everything except commercial and marketing."

He looks stricken.

"Partners. That's the word you used," she says. "You have to give it to me, all of it. No negotiations."

He shrugs, shakes his head, turns and walks away, down the corridor toward his office.

It's over, she thinks and she's disappointed. She wants it, she wants him to come back.

He turns back, comes to her. "It's a deal," he says quietly.

She can feel the adrenalin. "I want it on the record," she says, as calmly as she can manage. "The video guys are back in the studio. We'll get it in writing later."

"Let's get to the studio," he says. "We've got to get this out, right now." He touches her arm, almost pulls her toward the video suite. She slips free of him, pulls her cell phone out, presses a contact-dial.

"One more thing, Sheldon."

She hands him the phone. He looks at the name onscreen, looks back at her, slumps his shoulders, puts the phone to his ear.

"Hi, no it's not Kjersti. It's Sheldon. Listen, Frank. I made a mistake. Things are changing here and... well. Frank, we want you back. I want you back. OK? No time right now to explain. I'm sorry. I'm really, genuinely sorry."

He hands the phone back to Kjersti. She smiles, speaks to Frank. "Just get off your arse and come to work, Frank. I'll explain everything. We've got a lot of work to do."

ABOUT THE AUTHOR

Colin Campbell is a video game journalist based in Santa Cruz, CA.
He has worked for multiple games magazines and websites, serving as
a writer, editor and publisher.

He is the recipient of the 2011 Games Media Legend Award and
the 2012 Good Games Writer of the Year.
Colin currently works as a senior reporter for Polygon.
More @colincampbellx.

WWW.PIRANHAFRENZY.COM

Made in the USA
Coppell, TX
29 November 2021

66680760R00083